I0823554

AN ARCHIVE OF ROMANCE

ALSO BY AVA REID

A Study in Drowning

Fable for the End of the World

A Theory of Dreaming

The Wolf and the Woodsman

Juniper & Thorn

AN ARCHIVE OF ROMANCE

HARPER
An Imprint of HarperCollins*Publishers*

HarperCollins Children's Books, a division of HarperCollins Publishers,
195 Broadway, New York, NY 10007

HarperCollins Publishers, Macken House,
39/40 Mayor Street Upper, Dublin 1, D01 C9W8, Ireland

An Archive of Romance

Special thanks to Blake Buesnel, Blake Hudson, and the Argosy Book Store.

harpercollins.com

Library of Congress Control Number: 2025939021
ISBN 978-0-06-346222-9—ISBN 978-0-06-348023-0 (special edition)

Typography by Julia Tyler
25 26 27 28 29 RRDSEA 10 9 8 7 6 5 4 3 2 1

First Edition

PART ONE

I had not known love, not truly—I had known only covetousness and passion. I had thought my head too loud for it and my heart too fearful of its own beating. Yet even with my poor head and my worried heart, love made its way to me. It is the inheritance of all human beings.

—FROM *ANGHARAD* BY ANGHARAD MYRDDIN (NÉE BLACKMAR), 191 AD

It began as all things did:
a girl on the shore, terrified and desirous.

The sea called to me, as it does to so many, a thing both wretched and divine, both beautiful and terrifying. Being a far way from my home, and of little interest to my father and my sisters, I visited the shore alone, tasting the salt air and feeling the brooding mists of my own solitude. Cold wind beat and enveloped me by turns; the tide rose and then ebbed, pulling at my bare feet and then leaving me bereft.

just like the Fairy King

her loneliness makes her vulnerable

I plucked up pretty shells, admiring them for a moment and then tossing them into the foaming surf, only to have them returned to me when the water rushed back. I played at being a mermaid princess, imagining my sodden dress a tail, my tangled hair a crown. But for all my florid dreaming, I never dared to wade farther into the sea than up to my knees. I was as frightened by the pull of the tide as my own wanting of it; I had some perilous, strange desire to drown.

To the esteemed students of the Architectural College,

The estate of Llyr's national author EMRYS MYRDDIN is soliciting designs for a manor home outside the late author's hometown of Saltney, Bay of Nine Bells.

We ask that the proposed structure—HIRAETH MANOR—be large enough to house the surviving Myrddin family, as well as the extensive collection of books, manuscripts, and letters that Myrddin leaves behind.

We ask that the designs reflect the character of Myrddin and the spirit of his enormous and influential body of work.

We ask that the designs be mailed to the below address no later than midautumn. The winner will be contacted by the first day of winter.

Chapel
Architecture College
Administrative Building
Dean's Residence
Statue of Sion Billows
Literature College
Former Astronomy College
Swear Fealty
Lake

University of Llyr
Music College
Faculty Residence
Student Housing
Fine Art College
Library
Auxiliary Library
History College
Theater
Student Housing
Drowsy Poet
Sleeper Museum
TO NO CAUSE BUT KNOWLEDGE
B A L A

The SLEEPER

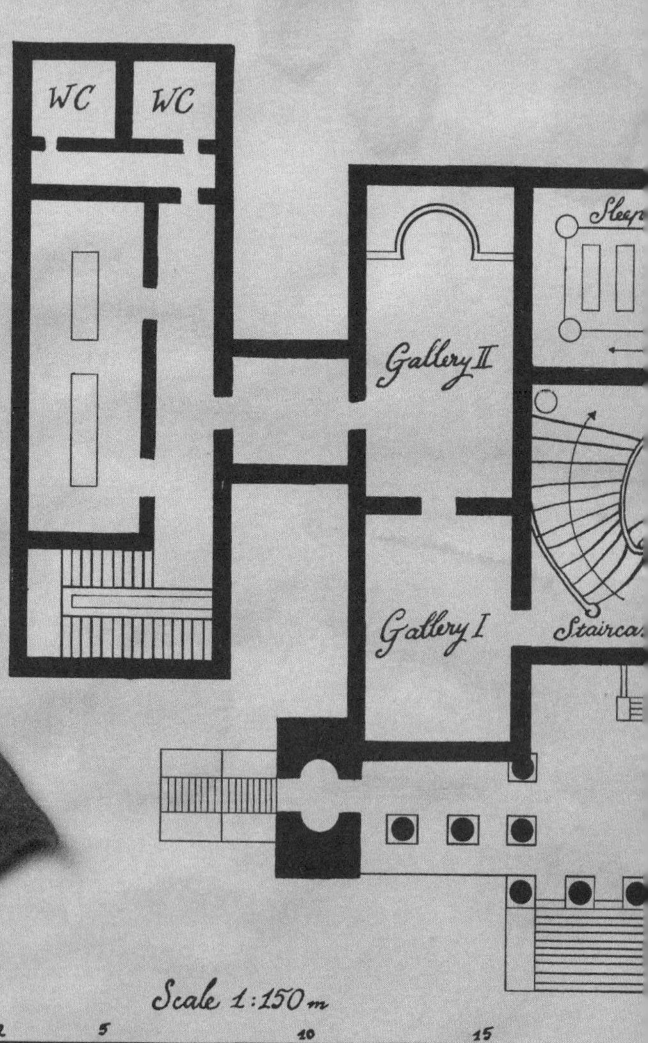

Scale 1:150 m

1 2 5 10 15

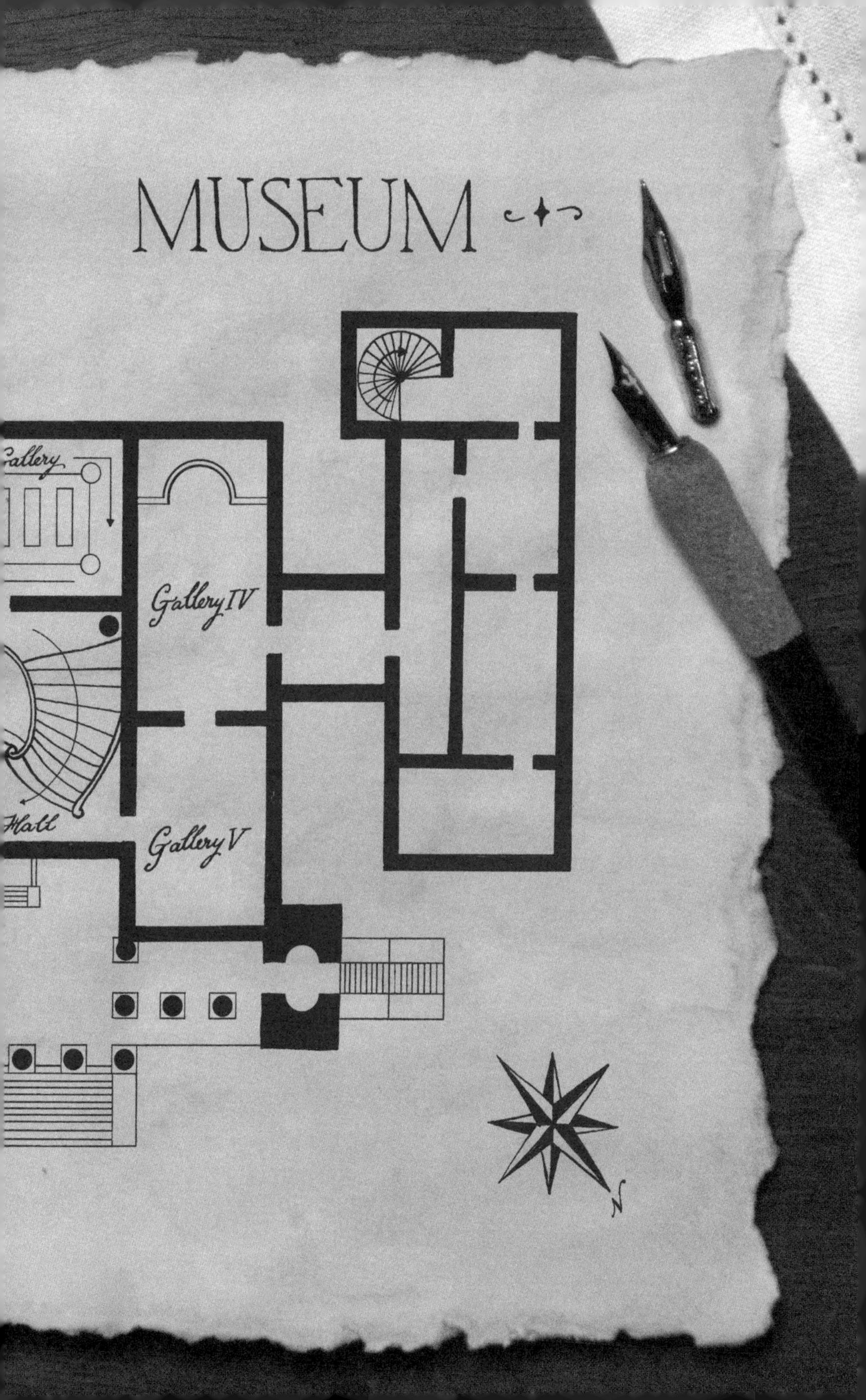

MUSEUM

Gallery

Gallery IV

Hall

Gallery V

Fairy rings are a phenomenon nearly exclusive to the South of Llyr, and have been overwhelmingly found in the most rural of areas, in forest glades or upon the open moors. A fairy ring is a circle of curious white mushrooms, stones, or other plants of mysterious origin, arranged as though by an intentional hand. According to some local legends, these are portals between the mortal world and the realm of the Fair Folk; other lore presents them as locations where fairies have used their magic and made a mark upon the land. Either way, they are places that are dangerous to humans, and every local I encountered told me that I ought to stay clear of them, their voices full of dire warning.

THE FAIR FOLK: AN ETHNOGRAPHY
DR. ATTICUS SEGRAVE

And indeed I encountered many of the Fair Folk on my journey into the woods or onto the moors—pale, beautiful creatures who spoke in riddles, who danced in the moonlight, who plied me with fae wine and false oaths. My fellow scholars have dismissed me as mad. But this is the truth; I swear it upon every saint worshipped by man.

Kitchen
Drawing room
Ante-chamber
WC
Atrium
Dining room
Library
Cloak room
Vestibule
Vera
GROUND FLOOR

HIRAETH MANOR

(REDESIGN)

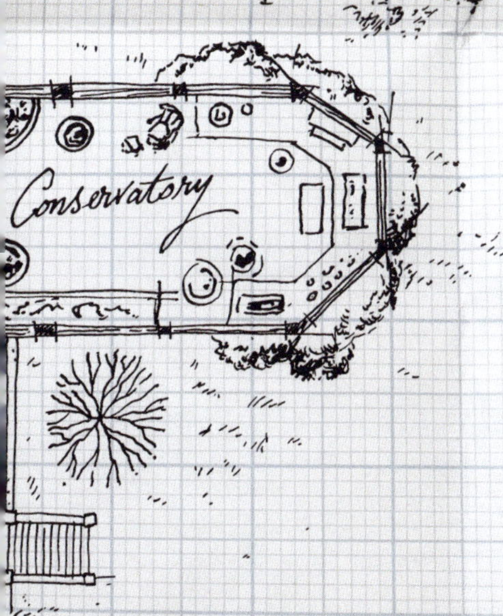

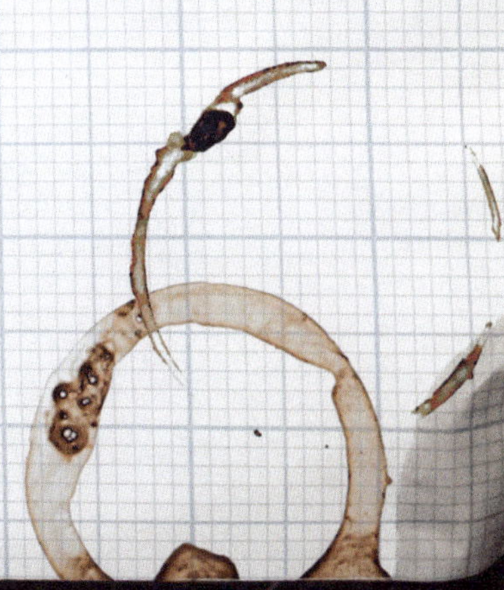

Once he began appearing to me—in wisps of smoke, in slants of shadow—I searched desperately for any methods to keep him at bay. I ate nothing but bread and salt, filling my belly with that which repelled immortal creatures, and whittling myself down to bone, to make my body more like a girl, less like a woman. (Fool I was to think this would repulse him!) I hung at my father's door silver bells; around my bed I set boughs of mountain ash. I read, in some ancient text of my father's, that ash trees are imbued with the blessings of the saints. And I fashioned for myself, crudely, an iron girdle, which I wore each night when I slept. Iron is bane to the Fair Folk. This, everyone knows.

ISSUED TO	BOOK TITLE
P. Héloury	Emrys Myrddin: A Life
P. Héloury	The Origins of a Sleeper: Myths and Truths About Emrys Myrddin
P. Héloury	Beyond "Angharad": A Biographical Reading of the Works of Emrys Myrddin
P. Héloury	A Boy from the Bay: The Childhood of Emrys Myrddin

EMRYS MYRDDIN

is the author of *Angharad* and *The Youthful Knight*, as well as selected poems. He lives in Saltney, Bay of Nine Bells, with his wife and son.

Greenebough Publishing

The
DROWSY POET
Menu
TEA DRINKS
Black .... 1.25 si
With milk .... 2.00 sil
COFFEE
Black .... 1.50 silvers
With milk .... 2.25 silvers
SCONE PASTRY
(blueberry, raspberry, plain) 1.50 silvers
MUFFIN
(blueberry, lemon, chocolate) 3.5 silvers
PROVIDE YOUR TICKET TO THE
SLEEPER MUSEUM FOR 25% OFF

THE KINGDOM OF
LLYR
SALTNEY
BAY OF
NINE BELLS
THE BOTTOM
HUNDRED
LALESTON
DRAEFEN
RIVER NAER
SYFADDON
Penrhos
Blackmar Estate

W
S
N
E
CAER-ISEL
KER-IS
LAKE BALA
THE COUNTRY OF
ARGANT
Map of
ARGANT
and
LLYR

Dear Ms. Sayre,

I am writing to congratulate you on the selection of your proposal for the design of Hiraeth Manor. I received a great many submissions, but yours was far and away the one I felt best honored my father's legacy.

I happily invite you to Saltney, to speak with you in person about your design. By the end of your stay, I would hope to have a set of finalized blueprints so we can break ground on the project swiftly.

To get to Hiraeth, please board the earliest train from Caer-Isel to Laleston, and then switch to the train bound for Saltney. I apologize in advance for the long and arduous journey. I will have my barrister, Mr. Wetherell, pick you up at the station.

With greatest enthusiasm,

Ianto Myrddin

Elegy for a Siren

What is a mermaid but a woman half-drowned,
What a selkie but an unwilling wife,
What a tale but a sea-net,
Snatching up both from the gentle tumult of dark waves?
There, in the shipless waters, I see her,
Skin gleaming like an oyster's pearl,
Seaweed woven in her hair.
She floats, she dives, unmoored from time.
I toss my rope (a noose, a lifeline)—
As startled as a woken sleeper,
She turns, she gasps,
Pricking up her pale fey ears.
Her arms are white and breach the waves,
As I wait, a hunter near upon a deer.
She swims, in trails of rainbow foam,
And stills before my craft.
I reach for her, she reaches back,
Her soft flesh cringing beneath
My rugged sailor's grasp.
She cannot speak; nor can I.
But in the mist, among the salt,
The story bends and warps
Like the wood of an ocean-weary craft,
And holds us in its supple hand.

FIRST CLASS
DISTRICT RAILWAY
HOLDER OF TICKET
Name: Effy Sayre
Route: Laleston to Saltney
THIS TICKET IS NOT TRANSFERABLE, AND MUST BE GIVEN UP, AT THE LATEST, ON THE DAY AFTER THE TERM FOR WHICH IT IS ISSUED EXPIRES, OTHERWISE THE DEPOSIT PAID ON IT WILL BE FORFEITED.
58276
S.

The Llyrian Times

"The finest, printed."

Vol. CLXIV | Seventh Day of Spring | Price: 1 Silver

Emrys Myrddin Dead at 84

It is with the heaviest of hearts that we report the death of Emrys Myrddin, author of *Angharad*. According to his barrister, Mr. Thomas Wetherell, he passed peacefully in his sleep, of natural causes, at the age of eighty-four.

In his final years, Myrddin retreated entirely from public life, sequestering himself in his estate in Saltney, Bay of Nine Bells. He took no interviews and entertained no guests. However, despite his self-imposed exile, his second novel, *Angharad*, has become one of the most commercially successful and beloved books in all of Llyr's history and has made him an instant candidate for Sleeper status upon his death.

Neither the Sleeper Museum nor the Llyrian Ministry of Culture responded to our requests for comment. In a prepared joint statement, the museum and the ministry said, "We recognize the immense contributions that the late Mr. Myrddin has made to Llyrian literature, and we offer our sincerest condolences to his family."

Myrddin is survived by his wife and son, neither of whom could be reached for comment. There have been no public announcements of funeral proceedings, leading many to speculate that arrangements are being made to inter him in the Sleeper Museum. While that remains to be seen, this paper's editorial staff shares in the nation's collective grief and celebrates the achievements of one of Llyr's greatest men.

I waited for the Fairy King in our marriage bed, but he didn't know I wore a girdle of iron.

Every night he came to me, and sometimes it was tender. It was not so much that his viciousness was suppressed—he would never think to disallow himself anything, not even a sentiment—but that he enjoyed tenderness for its own sake. Strange to say, I know, but though he was immortal, though he was powerful beyond my comprehension, he was still a man. There were moments when he wished for me to care for him, as any wife would her husband. When I stroked his hair and it did not feel damp, when I touched his face and it did not feel cold. When his flesh gave slightly beneath my hands.

That night, he came to me seeking such tenderness.

For a moment I thought it might sway me from my course. His shoulders were slumped, as though the day had wearied him. There was some invisible burden he bore, as an ox does its load. It was Arethusa's loss, perhaps, that he still grieved. It was the child in my belly that had been lost to us both—though he did not know by what secret means.

"Darling girl," he said, and his voice was low. His crown faltered on his brow.

Was I cruel, to do it now? When his knees trembled beneath him? When he came to me for comfort, and not for passion? I still wonder, even now.

"My love," I whispered in return.

A MEDITATION ON WATER AND FEMININITY IN THE WORKS OF EMRYS MYRDDIN

Many of the same themes, motifs, and symbols pervade Emrys Myrddin's works, from his poetry to his famous novel *Angharad*. Where they are notably absent is his first novel, *The Youthful Knight*, a tale of chivalry that bears more in common with classic epic romances such as Perceval ab-Owain's *Corentin and the Knight of the Greene*. *The Youthful Knight* has historically been understudied, perhaps because it bears such little similarity to his later, and more acclaimed, work.

Perhaps the most salient motif of all in Myrddin's work is water. His biographical details may help explain his fascination: he was born a fisherman's son in the Bottom Hundred; the sea was both his livelihood and, potentially, his ruin. Little else is known about his family and his early life.

Myrddin's depiction of women is also notable for both its vastness and its complexity. In "Elegy for a Siren" (Myrddin 184), the titular siren is presented as the quarry, both romantic and sexual, of the sailor. Her "feyness" excites the narrator with a fascination that borders on predation. And yet the poem is aware of this fact and subtly chastises the sailor for his base desires: her soft flesh "cringes [sic]" beneath his "rugged sailor's grasp" (Myrddin 184).

We must discuss, then, the relationship between women and water. When men fall into the sea, they drown. When women meet the water, they transform. It becomes vital to ask: Is this a metamorphosis or a homecoming?

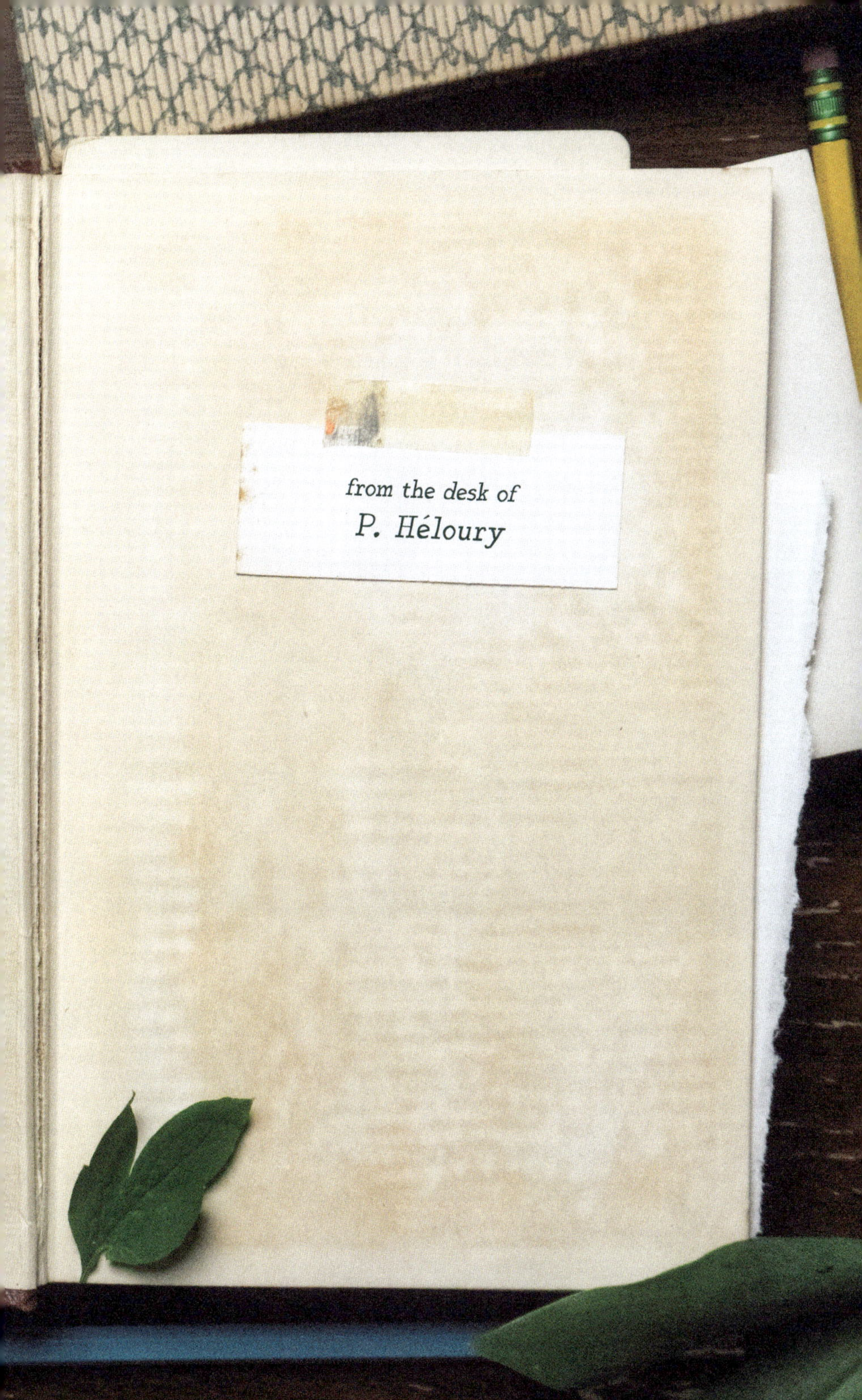
from the desk of
P. Héloury

another guest at Hiraeth Manor today. Ianto told me nothing about her other than that she is a student at the university—in the architecture college. And then, with the look of vague repulsion that I've become accustomed to, he woke me up at the earliest hour of dawn and ordered me to fetch her from the guesthouse.

He didn't see fit to sufficiently warn me that she is Emrys Myrddin's greatest admirer. But there was no way for me to know that she had seen my name on the library log. Or that she would have such an impossible temper. She is infuriatingly passionate and startlingly sharp-tongued. A girl who's come to build a house on a sinking foundation. To turn a ruin into a wonder.

The defiance in her gaze was difficult not to match. She glared at me from across the clifftop, wind lashing her long golden hair. I don't like how easily she riled me. This blue-blooded Llyrian girl, with her lilting accent, improper clothes, and pert little nose. Who purportedly studies architecture but gave me an impressively eloquent, if snarling, upbraiding about Myrddin's work and legacy.

Stupid to be daunted for even a moment by this posh Llyrian girl with a ribbon in her hair. But her eyes were unrelenting. And very green.

She really was completely improperly dressed. I had the equally improper urge to offer her my coat.

If she manages to find out my true purpose here, I doubt I'll survive her fury. Ianto is already suspicious enough; I've no desire to involve myself with her further. What would be the point? Our purposes here—and indeed, even our views on scholarship itself—are diametrically opposed. Any conversation would end in argument. I dislike being provoked to anger, or over-defensiveness.

Best for me to stay away from her. I want her out of my way and out of my head. She has taken up too much of my time—and my thoughts—already. I find myself vexed by so many questions: Why has she come here, to fulfill this impossible task? Why did Ianto choose her, a first-year, only a few weeks into the architecture program? Surely there were better-suited candidates. And why does she speak with more passion about literature than about her chosen field?

All of this rumination is pointless. She's a prim, blond, and clearly affluent Northern girl. (Given this, I have to admit she's rather brave to have come here alone. Hiraeth frightens even me sometimes, and so does Ianto.) She thinks with emotion rather than with reason. To her, I'm an arrogant Argantian interloper. We have nothing in common, and I should not waste my efforts trying to find out more. We represent, to one another, everything that the other despises.

But . . . I do think I recognize her name. Effy Sayre. I've heard it before.

The "P. Héloury" on my notebook now feels treasonous. She has successfully put me off my own name. Ridiculous. I despise every sentiment she has roused in me.

The Mariner's Demise

Everything ancient must decay,
A wise man once said thus to me.
But a sailor was I—and on my head no fleck of gray—
So with all the boldness of my youth, I said,
"The only enemy is the sea."
No man escapes his primal fault,
That silent seep of black decay.
"Decay is one thing, danger another," I said—
laughingly.
But the wise men laughed right back at me and said,
"The sea is a thing no sword can slay."
Gray and white of beard he was,
That man so aged, so sage,
Like a child I was to him,
Charging to a black-mawed death.
His words, within me, provoked a rage.
I was not like those other men,
I shouted, I declared, I raved.
The sea to me was much like a bride
Her foam a grand lace veil
My foolish rabid thirst—and lust—I could not stave.

Introduction

There is hardly a task more enticing—or more vexing—than attempting to construct a biography of Emrys Myrddin. I, Dr. Cedric Gosse, of the University of Llyr, have written what is considered the consummate work on Myrddin's life—yet even it is a sparse tome, with many liberties taken. To fill in the significant gaps, I have weaved biographical facts with lines of poetry and samples of prose—assuming, rather boldly, I am aware, that all of Myrddin's work is to a great extent biographical.

Such interpretation is tempting, given the almost whimsical circumstances of Myrddin's life. A destitute boy from the Bottom Hundred, a lowly fisherman's son. A commercial failure of an author, whose first work would have otherwise been forgotten by history if not for the astounding and unexpected success of the second.

Myrddin's reception is as curious as the man himself. Some critics accuse him of excessive romanticism (see Fox, Montresor, et al.). Yet Angharad is grudgingly accepted, even by his detractors, as a profound and surprising work. His admirers—and there are many, both critical and commercial—insist that the relatability of his work, the universalism, is intentional, reflecting a keen understanding of the human condition. In this manner, he is generally considered worthy of his status as national author.

THE BLEATING SHEEP PUB
SALTNEY, BAY OF NINE BELLS
ORDER
1 x WHISKEY (NEAT) 4.5 silvers
1 x WHISKEY (NEAT) 4.5 silvers
TOTAL: 9.0 silvers
CUSTOMER SIGNATURE:
Preston Geloury
THANK YOU!

I've utterly failed in my efforts to keep my distance. But what was I supposed to do—let her stumble down the cliffs in the pouring rain? She could have fallen or frozen to death. She's as infuriatingly stubborn as she is compellingly clever.

I went to the pub again to work, though I couldn't find my focus. I owe Master Gosse a letter (or three), but I've been stymied over and over again by Ianto, and today, I couldn't stop thinking about her. Effy. Running over arguments in my mind.

When she joined me at the pub, I was too flustered—I know. She must suspect something by now. Perhaps I shouldn't have let her lure me into another debate. I should be better at keeping my head. But something about her makes the thoughts trip around in my mind.

On the car ride back, the sun parted faintly through the clouds. It shone through the car window and lit up her profile and, when she turned to me, her eyes. Their color is bright but deep at the same time. They remind me of something I can't quite place.

She noticed me staring. She was restrained enough not to say anything, but I know she did. From now on I'll keep away from her at all costs. I can't afford the distraction. I only wish I could stop thinking about the way her nose flares when she's frustrated, and the striking green shade of her eyes.

A Dirge for the Drowned

There is a seamy strip of land
Between water blue and cliff tops black
The air is mist, the sea is murk
And mortal eyes grow dim and hazed
From amidst the crash of waves,
The clouds that gauze the wound of moon
A sound rings out, silver and clear,
And only for few mortal ears
The bells, the bells—
A dirge for the drowned.

I came upon this poem of Myrddin's incidentally—I was searching for another work when I flipped past and it caught my eye. Not the entire poem itself, but the reference to the bells. It is clearly a reference to the common legend of the Bottom Hundred, the bells that give the Bay of Nine Bells its name. It's completely nonsensical, of course. Impossible. Ridiculous. Hiraeth—and sleeplessness—is doing strange things to my mind. But I cannot help wonder if Myrddin heard them, too.

The Drowning

The Drowning was more than a climatological event. It came to define social, political, and economic history in the region, and gave rise to a distinctive and ever-more-salient subculture among the residents of the Bottom Hundred. Somewhat paradoxically, it caused an upswing in Southern nationalism, a hardening of Llyr's North-South divide. It can thus be said that the Drowning structures the core of Southern identity, even nearly two centuries later.

This book was borne out of the weariness that many Southern academics, myself included, feel in our attempts to produce scholarship about the literary tradition of the South. I find that I am, if not directly stymied by my colleagues, then at least very often dismissed. There is little effort on their parts to connect Southern literary works to the economic, political, and climatological conditions of the South. There is even less acknowledgment of the juxtaposed realities of Northern vs. Southern life.

I intend for my book to be a consummate work on the subject, filling a void in literary scholarship. This book uses the Drowning as a framework for analyzing and understanding works of Southern literature, considering them inextricable. It therefore rejects, of course, any formalist reading of Southern literature, and provides a rare—and necessary—Southern perspective on these literary traditions.

This book includes not only my work but the work of other Southern academics—though few and far between we may be. I recognize that my colleagues may find this overly political and

TO DO:

- Check with Ianto about balconies and turrets. Perhaps he can give me a hint as to their age? Some of them might be able to be retained.

- Is there a way to test the soil around the manor and see how hard it is? Whether it can support a new foundation? I don't know. I should have brought some textbooks with me.

- Create a new sketch, from scratch. This will involve walking around the exterior of the property and taking notes on every angle and outline. I think . . .

- If I can somehow figure out how to preserve the building's existing foundation, Ianto will be more than pleased. I just don't know.

- I think M.C. was right. I have no idea what I'm doing here. I miss Rhia; I miss Caer-Isel. I should never have come.

- Maybe I can ask Preston if he knows where the closest library is. I could find some textbooks there.

Behind again. Ianto's lurking is quite the impediment.

Proposed thesis title? Execution of the Author: An Inquiry into the Authorship of the Major Works of Emrys Myrddin (Too antagonistic?)

Part one: present theory of false authorship, starting with ??

Part two: cryptographic evidence—ask Gosse for samples

Part three: letters, diary entries—use nearest mimeograph, in Laleston (Ask Ianto? Seems hopeless.)

As much as I'm reluctant to admit it, I'm at an impasse. The evidence exists—I'm certain of it—but how to get at it is another matter. Ianto is suspicious of my intentions, or he just finds me personally disagreeable. I can't write to Gosse. Not until I find something of significance.

Significance—~~A[illegible]ad's~~

Significance—golden hair, a crown (repeated on 223, 318)

Significance . . .

Effy

Effy

Effy

Effy

Effy

"I refuse mirrors," the Fairy King said. "I refuse them for me, and I refuse them for you. If you want to see what you are, look into the tide pools at dusk. Look into the sea."

And so I went down to the water and looked for myself in the tide pools at dusk, but that was another one of the Fairy King's jests. By the time it was dusk, the sun had cowed herself too much, drawn close to the vanishing horizon, and all that remained in those pools was darkness. Her waning light could not reach them.

I slapped at that cold, dull water with my hands, as if I could punish it for disobeying me. And in that moment, I realized that without knowing it, the Fairy King had spoken truly: although the tide pools had not shown me my face, I had been revealed. I was a treacherous, wrathful, wanting thing, just like he was. Just as he had always wanted me.

To Mr. Greenebough,

I have completed, at your request, the next quarter of the novel, and have enclosed that portion of the manuscript with this letter. I recall that you wished to make some edits—as you put it in your previous note, "so that it might be more appealing to the errant minds of the youths," and I hope you find that this extract is in line with your vision. I have added more tawdry details—and a bit more blood.

Yours sincerely,

Emrys Myrthin

She has found me out.

I was too careless, leaving scraps of my work around, writing in Llyrian. My frustration with this whole endeavor has made me imprudent and rash. I can't sleep. I can hardly eat. Nerves—it has to be. The knowledge that Ianto could be lurking around any corner . . .

And her. Effy. She'll help me, or so she says. I think she hopes to prove me wrong. Much as it pains me to admit it, she knows Myrddin better than I do. Me, with my eidetic memory, with three years of intensive study under the country's preeminent Myrddin scholar—

It isn't just that she has memorized all the words. She understands something deep and essential about "Angharad," something that eludes even me. We may be at odds in our thinking, but otherwise, in some ways . . . I could hardly have hoped for a better partner. Not that I plan on telling her that.

She deserves a place in the literature college. That much is without doubt. In some sense she may be a finer scholar than I. When her nostrils flare and her green eyes shine, I am starting to understand that I am about to be refuted.

I wish I didn't know what I know. I wish I had never heard her name before, carried through gossip and whispers. Whatever may or may not have taken place, the whispers are wrong. Effy Sayre is no vapid damsel. She is brilliant. And she might be the ruin of me yet.

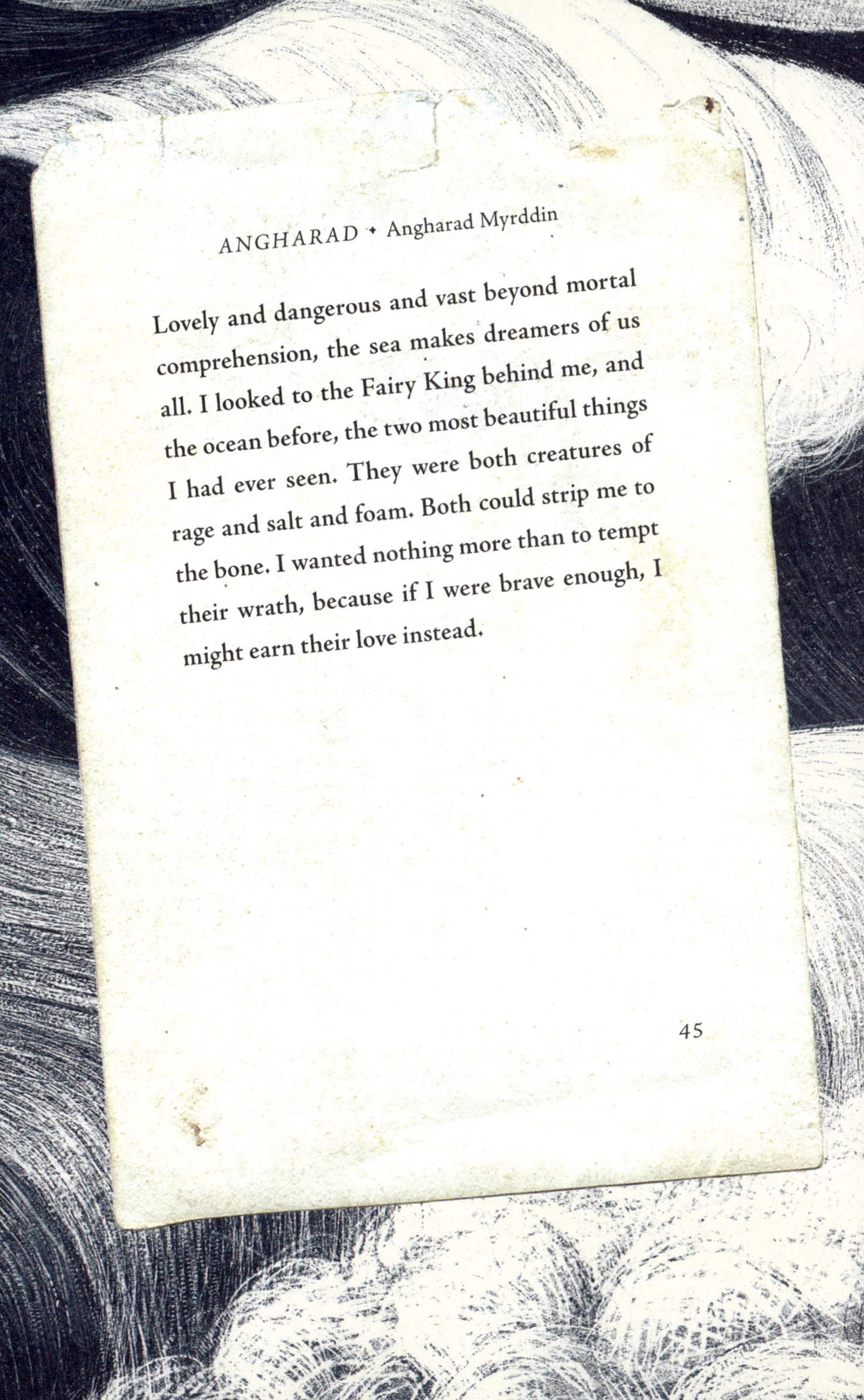

Lovely and dangerous and vast beyond mortal comprehension, the sea makes dreamers of us all. I looked to the Fairy King behind me, and the ocean before, the two most beautiful things I had ever seen. They were both creatures of rage and salt and foam. Both could strip me to the bone. I wanted nothing more than to tempt their wrath, because if I were brave enough, I might earn their love instead.

The Fairy King had many forms, and some looked, on the surface, identical. Some days I could not tell if the husband who came to me was the one who would kiss my eyes closed with infinite tenderness, or if he would press me down into our bed and not care that I whimpered. Those were the most difficult days. When I could not tell the kind version of him from the cruel. I wished he would be a serpent, a cloven-footed creature, a winged beast—anything but a man.

I myself had tried—in secret, of course—dabbling in his magic. Could I learn his arts of disguise, of transformation? Or were these powers beyond my capacity as a mere mortal? I did have my own methods of keeping him at bay: iron, rowan berries. Those were his weaknesses, but not his ruin. He faltered sometimes, but I knew he could not die.

Perhaps Arethusa could be of aid to me. In recent weeks, she had ceased to be so hostile to me. She had gone to silence, to seclusion. She was as quiet and cowed as any of my sisters, when they were punished for their insolence or indiscretion. Despite her dark hair and her uncanny, inhuman beauty, she reminded me of Marielle, my youngest. There was a certain vulnerability about her that I could not perceive when she openly despised me. Now I was aware of her slightness, how she was thinner, even, than I. How small she looked when she stood beside the Fairy King.

I went to her.

I must admit, I'd had my doubts when I accepted her alliance, but I hadn't considered that she would do such an utterly, confoundingly reckless thing as jumping out of a moving car.

Really! A moving car! At first I didn't believe her—she could have died, after all; the cliffs are already so perilous. That she managed to survive is a wonder; even more of a wonder is how she managed to walk all the way back to the manor by herself.

(But . . . I suppose I can't blame her. Not entirely. There are moments when I have felt the urge to do something similarly drastic in Ianto's presence.)

She's braver than I am. I've known it all along, in a way, but now I recognize it without a doubt. Brave to come to Hiraeth all alone, and to stay, even after she's seen the hopeless ruin of it, and to speak to Ianto as she does, without revealing anything. If anyone is going to give us away, it will be me. I'm a terrible liar. And far more given to nervousness and fretting.

I shouldn't have let her go alone. But I didn't know how to tell her that I was . . . worried, I suppose. I didn't want her to think I couldn't trust her. It's Ianto I don't trust. I'm not so naive that I don't see the way he looks at her. I hate myself, in some moments, for thinking the way he does. The thoughts flit through my mind before I can press them down. To deny that she's beautiful would be to deny the sea is salt. (Not that I will <u>ever</u> confess this. It will die as the shameful secret that it is).

But she's no ditsy damsel. I want her to know that I

believe in her even though I'm afraid. And I didn't know how to articulate my fear without telling her what I do know. About her, and that professor.

It preys on me, the knowledge. More and more with every passing day. Now that I've heard her laugh, felt her touch. Doctored her knee like some awkward, flustered schoolboy. After she left, I kept looking down at the blood on my hands, my skin prickling with heat. I have slept even less lately—no thanks to the sound of those infernal bells—and eaten almost nothing. I can't seem to want anything that I should.

When she stood above me, in the light filtering from the windows, setting her green eyes aglow, I realized what she reminds me of. There is a myth, in Argant, about a once-great city that sank beneath the waves. My father read it to me when I was a child, our heads nestled together against the pillows. I think it went something like this:

"But all was not lost, when the water swallowed Ker-Is. Under the sea, mermaids pray in the cathedral. Under the sea, fire burns green."

That's what she reminds me of. A fairy tale.

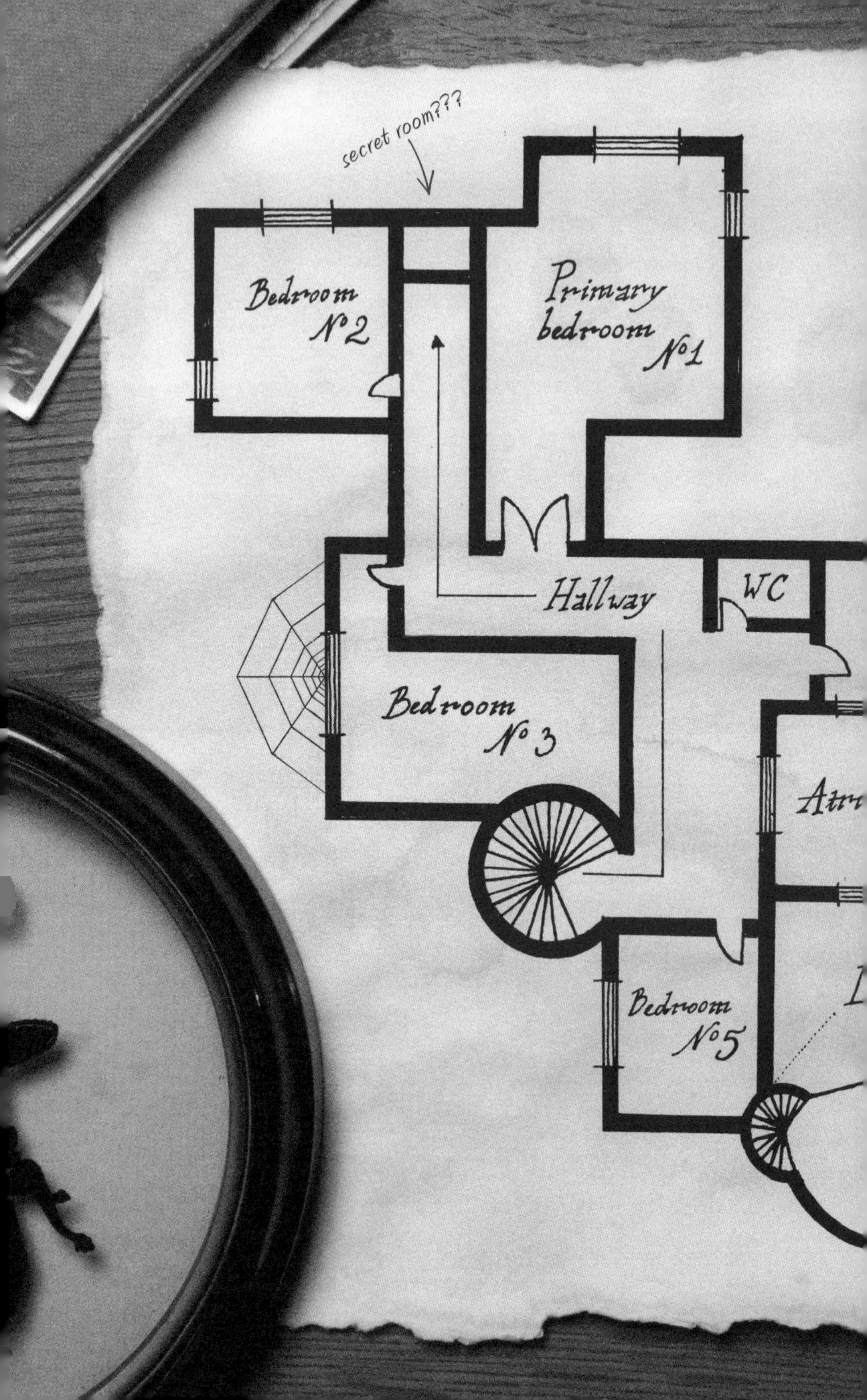
secret room???
Bedroom
№2
Primary
bedroom
№1
Hallway
WC
Bedroom
№3
Bedroom
№5

HIRAETH MANOR.

Saltney, Bay of Nine Bells.

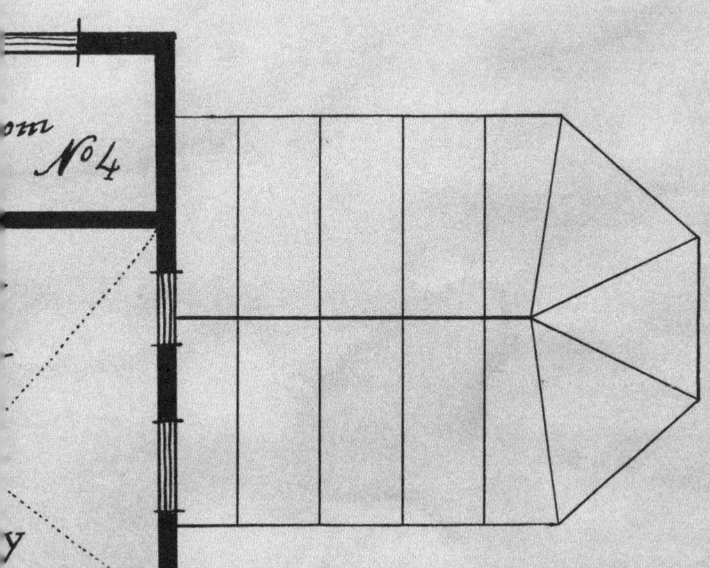

SECOND FLOOR.

Scale 1:150 m

1 2 5 10 15

I'm not entirely sure how she convinced me to come out, to risk death at no more than a clumsy bootstep. Somehow, her near tumble down the cliffs weeks ago has not sufficiently shaken her.

She walked out ahead of me, her golden hair streaming loose behind her. She'd not tied it back, perhaps realizing the futility of doing so with the wind so relentless at the top of the cliffs. When it blew back, the ends of it tickled my nose, and I found myself—frustratingly—thinking that I could touch it. That I could discover if it was as soft as it looked.

I should have been more concerned about falling to my death.

Effy paused on a very precarious-looking outcropping of stone and motioned for me to join her. It's a bit humiliating that I didn't even hesitate. Something about her makes me abandon all good sense.

We both stood there, at the edge of the cliffs, looking over the tumultuous and foam-choked sea. The sky above, a wedge of slate, its stillness almost perverse in contrast. No. Not perverse. Strange, but beautiful.

"This is what I wanted to see," she said. "What I wanted to show you."

"Believe it or not, I've become quite familiar with the sight of the ocean over the past few weeks."

She gave me a surly look. "Must you always be so stubbornly unsentimental?"

"If by unsentimental you mean pragmatic—"

"Oh, hush. Just look."

So I did. But not so much at the water—at her. Her cheeks and the tip of her nose, turning pink in the cold. Her eyes—green flame. Effy stared unblinkingly out at the water, seeing something that I could not. Was there a beauty, a poignancy there in the waves that's beyond my capacity to see?

A line came into my mind, the opening of "Angharad": "It began as all things did: a girl on the shore, terrified and desirous."

That below-water fire in her eyes. Fear and wanting, all at once. Very abruptly I felt the height in the soles of my feet.

"See?" Effy gestured. "This is what Myrddin must have seen. He must have stood here so many times and looked out over the waves. How could you not write something like 'Angharad,' when the sea looks like this to you? It's *magic*."

I almost told her, right then and there. About the bells.

Instead, I said, "Myrddin is far from the only man with a view of the ocean. Anyone in the Bottom Hundred could have seen the same magic."

Effy let out a breath. "You're insufferable."

But I did feel magic then—if magic means something that I can't explain, that I can't put into words. Only I didn't feel it when looking at the sea. I felt it when looking at her. This girl from the North, who loves the world like a naturalist, who speaks in the reverent tones of a poet, who seems somehow

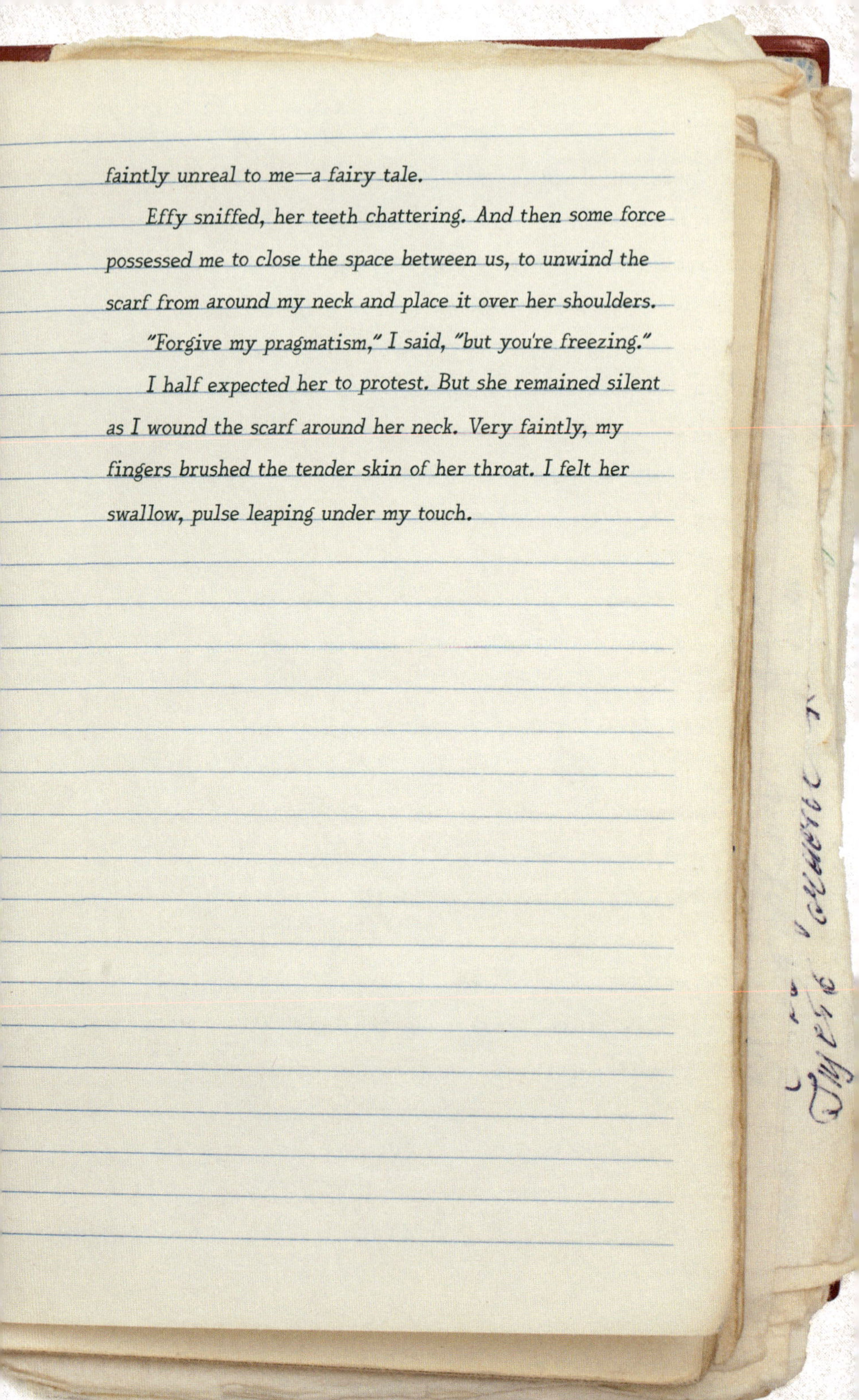

faintly unreal to me—a fairy tale.

Effy sniffed, her teeth chattering. And then some force possessed me to close the space between us, to unwind the scarf from around my neck and place it over her shoulders.

"Forgive my pragmatism," I said, "but you're freezing."

I half expected her to protest. But she remained silent as I wound the scarf around her neck. Very faintly, my fingers brushed the tender skin of her throat. I felt her swallow, pulse leaping under my touch.

Great Captain and His Sea-Bride

I can hear the mermaids singing
Beneath the rolling, wanton waves,
Their hair as lush as meadowsweet,
Their maidenheads as ripe for plunder
As the gold inside their sunken chests.

I will love you
to ruination

"I will love you to ruination," the Fairy King said, brushing a strand of golden hair from my cheek.

"Yours or mine?" I asked.

The Fairy King did not answer.

I did not press him. I felt the pulsing of his love then, both cold and warm, the heavy dampness before a winter storm. Because he had always told me he cherished my stubbornness, I went on instead, "How might such an immortal being come to ruin?"

A smile, as beautiful and sinister as it had ever been.

"Sly girl," he said. "Let me hold some of my secrets."

"A husband and wife should have no secrets from each other."

The Dreams of a Sleeping King

Colin Blackmar

When the king was first interred,
He did not dream at all.
It was the abhorrent nothingness
That cast a dreadful pall.
That bleak and black oblivion
Was too much like death to bear.
And so the dreams came like a balm
For the half-dead king's despair.
The dreams were not of mortal fare,
No idle whims and shallow yens.
No saints were beseeched with prayer.
Instead, he dreamed, once and again,
Of the feats of greatest man.
The lusty passions, the cold commands,
His banners and his steel.
His own wise brow, wrinkled frown,
And brazen bells that peal.

Another appearance of the myth, though more veiled here. Perhaps this has to do with Blackmar's "Southern fascination." He mines the legends of the South more blatantly than perhaps any other Northern writer. But there is the luster of Argant as well. My father had a book of fairy tales—I remember the story of Ys.

I'm going mad.

10 March 188

Visited Blackmar at Penrhos. He gave me some notes on *The Youthful Knight*, which were good. He also offered to introduce me to his publisher, some Mister Marlowe, in Caer-Isel. Blackmar seemed to think the head of Greene-bough Books would be charmed by my impoverished upbringing—what he called, a bit too self-importantly, my "rough edges." Three of his daughters were there as well. The wife, I assume, banished.

30 January 189

The Youthful Knight will be published. Greene-bough appears cautiously optimistic, but I do not expect much success. The youths themselves may read it, but I think it is too dry a tome. What do youths these days care for chivalry and modesty? Not very much, as far as I can tell. When I visited Penrhos I saw Blackmar's daughters again. The eldest is very fair and took an interest in my work. But a woman's mind is too frivolous, and though she was an unusually sober example of her sex, I could tell she was more preoccupied with dance halls and boys. She has written a few poems of her own.

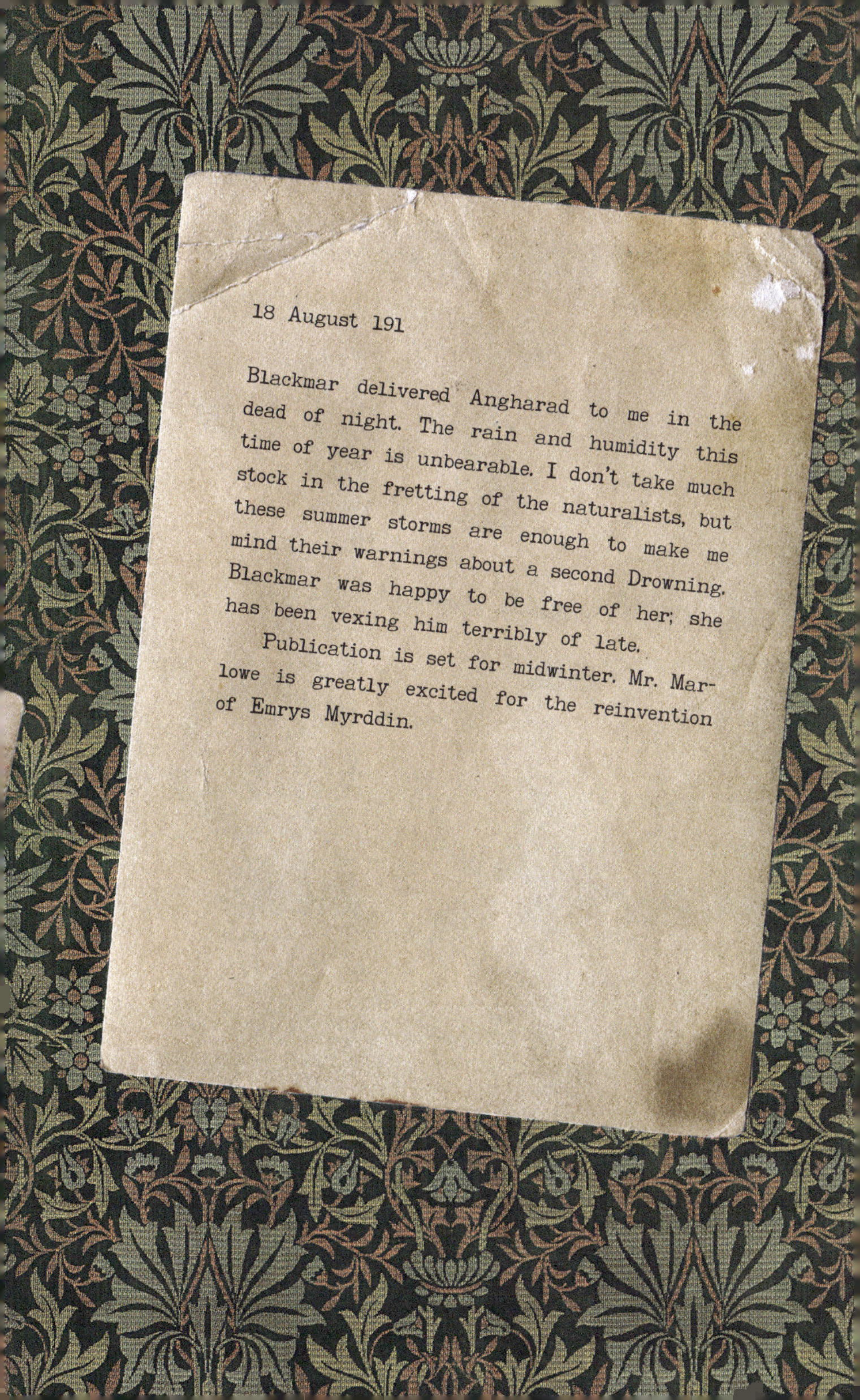
18 August 191

Blackmar delivered Angharad to me in the dead of night. The rain and humidity this time of year is unbearable. I don't take much stock in the fretting of the naturalists, but these summer storms are enough to make me mind their warnings about a second Drowning. Blackmar was happy to be free of her; she has been vexing him terribly of late.

Publication is set for midwinter. Mr. Marlowe is greatly excited for the reinvention of Emrys Myrddin.

Dear Mr. Blackmar,

I am a literature student at the university in Caer-Isel, and my thesis concerns some of the works of Emrys Myrddin. I've recently become aware that the two of you maintained correspondence, and I hoped I might make a scholarly inquiry into the nature of your relationship. I am happy to make the journey to Penrhos if you find face-to-face conversation preferable to written correspondence.

Sincerely,

Preston Héloury

Oh, you're hopeless. Watch.

Dear Mr. Blackmar,

I am so humbled and delighted to be writing to you. My name is Euphemia Sayre, and your poem "The Dreams of a Sleeping King" is enormously meaningful to me. I have loved it ever since I was a little girl. I still have my marked-up copy from primary school, which I brought to my university dormitory.

I was even more astonished and awestruck to learn that you were a good friend and confidant of Emrys Myrddin—another one of my favorite authors. You must have the most fascinating and amusing stories of your time together!

I am a student at the University of Caer-Isel, working on a project about Emrys Myrddin with a fellow student of mine. I hoped that I might be able to visit you at your estate and [illegible] more about you, your work, and your late friend. [illegible] ch I am curious about, and it would be a privilege [illegible] from an author I do so admire.

[illegible] most earnestly for your time, and for your [illegible] poem.

Sincerely,

Euphemia Sayre

I was a girl when he came for me, beautiful and treacherous, and I was a crown of pale gold in his black hair.

Water finds its way through the smallest spaces and narrowest cracks. Where the bone meets sinew, where the skin is split. It is treacherous and loving. You can die as easily of thirst as you can of drowning.

And drown I would, in his ruinous love, if I stayed. It both nourished me and reminded me horribly of my own emptiness. I had known nothing of such love before; how could I have known? Girlhood is meant for whimsy and quick-passing fancies. Not for these nightmares and scraping hungers.

I paced and paced, across that small room, contained like a bird in its cage. To escape was almost the easier part. First I would have to imagine that I could. First I would have to allow myself to dream.

Miss Euphemia Sayre,

I was pleased to receive such an admiring letter. You seem like a lovely, agreeable young woman. I would be more than happy to host you and your academic compatriot at my manor, Penrhos. You already know the address, as the successful delivery of your letter demonstrates. You seem like quite a special young girl indeed, to be so interested in the work of two old men, one now six months dead. I will certainly entertain you for as long as it takes to satisfactorily answer your questions about my work and the work of Emrys Myrddin. He was a dear friend and even, in the end, family.

All my best,

Colin Blackmar

I did not lose myself at once to anguish and despair. I refused. Perhaps it was the foolish boldness of girlhood, which makes us not fear the things we ought. After the third night he came to me, his shadow massed just beyond my door, I sat upright and tried to match his stare. His eyes were like knifepoints in the darkness, a shade so depthless and blacker than black.

He retreated with the rising of the sun, when the light soaked the world once more. And I went downstairs, stepping over my boughs of mountain ash, to the breakfast table with my silent mother and giggling sisters and my father, who reigned always like a petty lord.

"I saw him again," I said.

My sisters scarcely looked up from their gossiping. My mother's limpid gaze flickered to mine and her expression did not change. It was only my father who let out a low breath, threaded with impatience, and replied, "You had a dream."

"Yes, perhaps," I said. "But I was awake."

"Speak plainly. I've no patience for riddles."

I had always thought my father such a clever man. Another fantasy of girlhood, which I had also quickly shed. My voice rose, and I said, "He was there. Come to my bedroom at night and you will see him, too."

My father beat his palm against the table, with such force and suddenness that the silverware leaped up and then clattered down. My mother flinched. My sisters gasped.

"Enough of this," he growled. "You are not a child anymore."

Most scholars of Myrddin view him as somewhat in conversation with Blackmar, though the extent to which their work bears any genuine thematic or stylistic similarities is still debated. While Myrddin, in what few interviews he gave, was adamant that he did not seek to be known as a "Southern writer," Blackmar, though a Northerner himself, was very much inspired by the aesthetic and folkloric traditions of the South. In this paper, I argue that Blackmar perceived the South as a fanciful realm of whimsy, trapped in a time long past, existing merely for Northern writers to project their fantasies upon. In that regard, I contend that Blackmar is indeed a Southern writer—but only in the South of his own imagining.

The first section of this paper will cover the biographical details of Colin Blackmar. He was the first child of Rolant Blackmar and Letitia Heathcote, the former a self-made railroad magnate best known for expanding rail lines from the North to more remote and previously inaccessible areas of the South. Blackmar was born at the newly constructed estate of his father—which would later be named Penrhos—and was educated at St. Artegall's, the region's most prestigious boarding school.

Blackmar was a latecomer to the field of literature—interviews with his former classmates and teachers revealed that he was an unexceptional pupil, more inclined to the rugby field than to the library. It is believed that his mother was the one to impress upon him the importance of an education in literature, though this is unconfirmed and still debated. Whatever the cause, Blackmar ultimately enrolled in the literature college at the University of Llyr.

An Epistemological Theory of Romance

by Dr. Edmund Huber

What defines a romance? All scholars seem to converge on a single point: it is a story that must have a happy ending. And why is that? I say, it is because a romance is a belief in the impossible: that anything ends happily. For the only true end is death—and in this way, is romance not a rebuke of mortality? When love is here, I am not. When love is not, I am gone. Perhaps a romance is a story with no end at all, where the end is but a wardrobe with a false back, leading to stranger and more merciful worlds.

17 April 189

My sly and clever girl,

You must have gotten my address from papers in your father's study, or else how would you know where to write me? I shall not underestimate your shrewdness again, and perhaps I shall even expect you, one day, to show up at my door. I would not protest it. I might be very happy to see you scowling at me in the threshold.

The poems you sent me were, I think, rather good. I particularly enjoyed the one about Arethusa. I did not think a girl of Northern blood would have any interest in our myths and legends, but I suppose your father did not give you a Southern name for nothing.

Please do send me more, should you feel so inclined. When I am at Penrhos again, I would very much like to discuss Arethusa. She is generally seen as an aspect, or rather, an equivalent of Saint Acrasia who, as you know, is the patroness of seductive love. A very interesting subject for your poem.

Yours,

E.M.

13 November 189

My foolish and lovely girl,

I fear your father has discovered us. He asked me, without euphemism or subterfuge, where I had imperiled his daughter's purity, whether I had taken you to bed. I told him truthfully that we had NOT lain together. I don't know whether you are a virgin, like your self-styled protagonist. And I don't know why your father has such a keen interest in his daughter's purity—you are a grown woman, for Saints' sakes.

Best not to see each other for a while—at least until I can speak with your father about this delicate matter. But if you do manage to slip away, I shall reward you lavishly.

Yours,

E.M.

1 March 190

My beautiful and debauched girl,

You said something to me last night, as we lay together, that I shall not soon forget. I was near to sleeping, but you pulled the covers over your naked breast and sat up. Leaning over me, you said, "I will love you to ruination."

I sat up as if I had been prodded, since neither of us had said those three words to the other before, and answered somewhat groggily, "Whose ruination? Yours or mine?"

You did not answer, and still I wonder.

Yours (in every conceivable fashion),

E.M.

would return soon. We did not have much time. We waded through the rising waters, rough with salt, me clumsy in my mortal body, and her—

I turned and realized she was not following.

I moved back through the water as quickly as I could, slowed by its sucking torpor. My gown clung to me, as gossamer as spider silk. I returned to her where she stood, shivering, her skin sallow and her eyelashes fluttering.

"Come," I said, though I could not make my voice rise to surety and boldness. It trembled, as she did. "We're so close now."

Her dark hair fell about her shoulders, half-obscuring her face, her lovely form now thin and gaunt.

I had the hubris of a mortal, too. Still. Always. She was of this world and could not leave it. A creature of salt and foam, just like the Fairy King himself. She could not exist in the realm of banal humanity.

She touched her forehead to mine, wild-haired, fey creature that she was, an enemy to me once, as sly and unrelenting as the sea. Her flesh was cold, as it had always been, yet grew colder by the moment.

"Arethusa—" I began.

"No," she whispered. Water clung to her pale, parched lips, a cruelty, a perversion. "Go now. You must."

I closed my eyes and felt her touch recede, like the ebbing of the tide. When I opened them again, she was gone. Dissipated, blown like ash on the wind. My erstwhile ally. My friend.

SONG: The Maiden of the North
(For Elinore)
ALBUM: Idylls & Canticles
ARTIST: Alby Camaret
FIRST STANZA:
There she comes,
On a lily-white steed
Her hair from its ribbon freed
Loosed by the winds that
Trip the borderline
A maiden so fair,
The truest love of mine

I only pretended to sleep, keeping my eyes closed until I heard her breathing steady into the rhythm of slumber. Then I opened my eyes and watched her: hair strewn out gold against the covers, the pale curve of her throat, her collarbones. More of her skin than I've ever seen before.

I wrote her name on that paper because I thought it might exorcise my wanting from me. Effy Effy Effy Effy Effy. Each repetition a confession. A plea for release. I sat so many times in that dark booth as a child, the priest's face obscured by the screen between us. At my mother's prodding, I confessed to a child's crimes. White lies, lies by omission, breaking one of my brother's toys.

I wonder what a priest would recommend to absolve me of this greatest transgression. It's sinful, how I think of her. How I imagine the way she would look, bare and keening beneath me.

I can't touch her. It would ruin us both. But my atheism, my skepticism, my pragmatism—it seems to all be crumbling. Like stone walls, struck over and over again by the waves.

"Ar mor a lavar d'ar martolod: poagn ganin, me az pero, diwall razon, me az peuzo"—Says the sea to the sailor: strive with me and live; neglect me and drown.

"Evit ar mor bezán treitour, treitouroc'h ar merc'hed"—The sea is treacherous, but women are even more treacherous.

"Ar gwir garantez zo un tan; ha ne c'hall ket berán en e unan"—Love is a fire that cannot burn alone.

Llyr's pantheon of saints has been the subject of much scholarly fascination over the centuries, among academics in the fields of both literature and history. A notable feature is that the qualities and the composition of the pantheon varies not as much across space as across time—where one might expect a stark divide between the Northern modes of worship and the Southern, there is instead a fairly cohesive conception of the saints throughout all of Llyr, with few minor regional distinctions.

The passage of time has shifted religious and spiritual ideals, with the various saints often being removed or modified beyond recognition. These changes frequently coincide with social, economic, and political transformations. While our knowledge of the earliest forms of the pantheon is scant, recent adaptations can allow us to "reverse-engineer" a timeline that tracks the shifts beginning in approximately 800 BD (Wilde 23).

Perhaps the most recent example of these "canon shifts" is the transformation of Acrasia and Amoret (Wilde 116). It is theorized that the goddesses Acrasia and Amoret were once a single female figure, rather than the two-headed goddess worshipped in Llyr today. When did Llyrians begin to see love as strictly dichotomic, rather than of a vast and multitudinous quality? Why was this dichotomy characterized by submission versus dominance? I put forth the argument that this doctrinal transformation is tied to the evolving role of women in Llyrian society, the fear of female advancement, particularly in the decades immediately following the Drowning.

I stared up at her, at the face that's surfaced in my every dream, at her green-fire eyes that made me wonder whether I've been wrong, and all the stories are right—the fairy-tale girl I would have knelt for, plucked up a sword for . . .

But this isn't a fairy tale, and I could hurt her as easily as I could love her.

I would never stop hating myself if I hurt her. I wanted more than anything to kiss her, but I restrained myself, at least in this. Instead I gathered her golden hair, which was falling over both of us, and tucked it behind her shoulders. The effort felt enormous. I wanted her so badly I could barely breathe. But she needed gentleness, so I pressed the desire down.

I held her as close to me as I dared. My wanting all ran through me, and then wrung me out, leaving me boneless and afraid. Afraid because I might have lost my chance. It was the first time I've held her, and it might be the last.

When she was gone, back to the guesthouse, I went downstairs. Vaguely aware that I should eat. The only thing that's touched my tongue in a day and a half is the end of a cigarette.

I was in the kitchen, searching for something passably edible, when Ianto appeared behind me.

"So Cedric Gosse's illustrious protégé does hunger like us mortals." There was no humor in his voice, only ice. "The

cabinets are rather bare, I'm afraid. Wetherell is making a trip to town tomorrow."

"I'll survive until then."

"Lucky for you, Hiraeth never runs dry." He opened one of the cabinets and produced a sticky-looking bottle of whiskey, half-full.

"No thank you," I said. "I'd rather go to bed."

But Ianto was already pouring us both a dram. "Nonsense. It's called a nightcap, Argantian."

I stiffened. Ianto thrust the glass into my hand. He watched me expectantly, unblinkingly, until I raised the glass to my lips and took a sip. He didn't look away until I swallowed.

I waited, but Ianto didn't lift his own glass. He merely watched, with those inscrutable gray eyes. Then he said, "She's a beautiful girl, isn't she?"

I tensed immediately, fingers clenching around the glass.

"I see how you look at her. I can hardly blame you. It's in a man's nature, to want to possess beautiful things."

"Speak for yourself," I replied.

Ianto's gaze lifted, the corner of his mouth twitching. "Are you truly convinced that you're above mortal desires?"

If only. I remember the feeling of her hips pressed against mine, the softness of her thigh under my hand, only the thin nylon of her stockings between my skin and hers.

Petulantly, vengefully—in so visceral a way that it almost shamed me, I thought: you'll never touch her like that.

"A man ruled by his instincts is a weak man," I said. "People aren't treasures to plunder."

Ianto smiled in a way that chilled my blood.

"Ever the aloof scholar," he said. "But words will not keep you warm at night. You'll need a woman for that."

It took all my restraint not to smash the glass across Ianto's face. If I were a weaker man—or maybe a stronger one—I would have.

Instead, I said, "I think I'll take my nightcap alone."

I did not grow in the mortal sense: my body changed little; my face took on no creases of age. It was only my hair that grew, long enough to brush my bare ankles, long enough that I might spend hours taming it into a series of braids. This had been Arethusa's task once. Now I worked with my own fingers.

Yet not always alone. The Fairy King was keen to watch, though he never offered his aid. It was difficult work without a mirror. He stood behind me, always wearing that expression of indulgent contempt.

Often he would tell me stories of those girls who had been in his bed before. Weak, he called some; others boring. One laughed too loudly and too solicitously. Another was as simpering and flighty as a moth. His tales slid between us like water through a crack in the wall.

"Were there really a thousand of them?" I asked once.

"No." His reply had a twist of humor in it. "They were not girls to me. They were prey. They were not like you."

I passed so many sleepless nights wondering how I could ever escape him. And yet I found the true fetters were ones of my own creation.

Those nights I kept circling the same ancient question: Why had the Fairy King chosen me? What had I done to deserve this?

That question was powerful magic indeed, for it kept me trapped there, my husband slumbering beside me. Until I broke the spell my mind had cast, I could not ever be free.

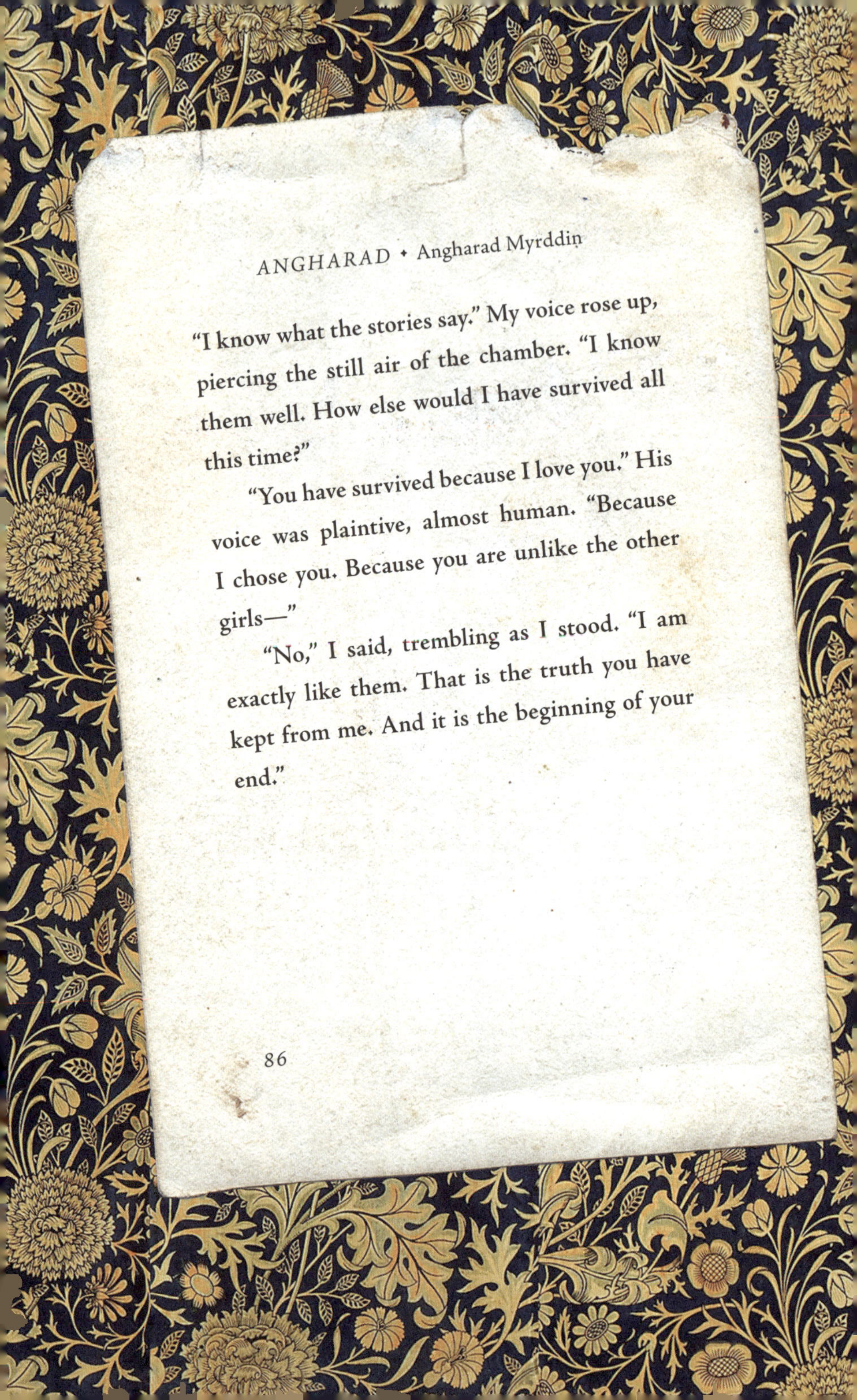

"I know what the stories say." My voice rose up, piercing the still air of the chamber. "I know them well. How else would I have survived all this time?"

"You have survived because I love you." His voice was plaintive, almost human. "Because I chose you. Because you are unlike the other girls—"

"No," I said, trembling as I stood. "I am exactly like them. That is the truth you have kept from me. And it is the beginning of your end."

What wisdom do you want from a death-marked girl? I can say only this: In the end I learned that the water was in me. It was a ghost that could not be exorcised.

But even a guest, uninvited, must be attended to. You make up a bed for them. You pour from your best bottle of wine. If you can learn to love that which despises you, that which terrifies you, you can dance on the shore and play in the waves again, like you did when you were young. Before the ocean is friend or foe, it simply is. And so are you.

Uncovering *Angharad*: An Inquiry into the Authorship of Major Works Attributed to Emrys Myrddin

By Euphemia Sayre and Preston Héloury

I INTRODUCTION

Despite its longstanding fame and near-legendary status in the collective cultural imagination of Llyr, the purported author of *Angharad*, Emrys Myrddin, has always been an enigma. Few photos of him exist, and even fewer interviews; the biographical information on the jacket flap of *Angharad* offers little glimpse into the character of the man, who retreated entirely from public life in his final years.

This paper, jointly authored, puts forth that Emrys Myrddin is not only an enigma but a fraud, whose works have been falsely attributed to him in a decades-long conspiracy involving prominent members of the literary community.

too forceful, perhaps?

The importance of this endeavor cannot be overstated. In the years following its publication, *Angharad*'s massive commercial success has greatly financially benefited key players in the conspiracy, such as Greenebough Publishing and its editors in chief, Kitteridge Marlowe and his late father. To accrue such profit under false pretense is not only a financial crime, prosecutable by law, but a betrayal of the trust of Greenebough's patrons and readers.

I don't think this matters as much as the other reasons—should we cut or move to the end?

Greenebough has always marketed *Angharad* alongside Myrddin himself: with great paternalism, the novel has been promoted as an example of Southern ingenuity, a rags-to-riches tale of an impoverished fisherman's son transcending his circumstances to author one of the most acclaimed and influential novels in history. Myrddin's biography is nearly as famous as *Angharad* itself, his legacy and character made even more intriguing by his reclusiveness in later years. This narrative has been absolutely crucial to Greenebough's marketing and publicity efforts.

And it has all been fiction.

Dear Miss Euphemia Sayre,

After having revisited your work and application materials, we are pleased to offer you a place in the university's literature college.

The excellence and prestige of the literature college depends entirely on the character and capabilities of the student body. In offering you admission, the university places its faith in you to uphold the virtues of learning and to offer meaningful contributions to the field of literature.

Please find attached all necessary materials and instructions for how to draw up your class schedule. We look forward to your attendance.

Sincerely yours,
The Hon. Quincy Fogg, Dean of the University of Caer-Isel

My return to the mortal world was not some simple thing. There was no path, cleared and neat. And I did not even have magic to guide me; the Fairy King had taken all gold and glittering and wondrous things with him. He had taken my dreams.

Yet I found my way, in the end. I left his manor as I had come, in my gauzy white nightgown, my feet bare. I felt the cool dampness of the grass, saw the morning dew, which sparkled in the leaves like so many bits of glass. I listened to the birds, trilling each to each, their wordless songs of ardor.

I walked and walked until I found that forgotten place. The fairy ring: a circle of strange-growing mushrooms in the grass. Here the birdsongs were silent. No animals rustled in the green.

And I waited there until my legs quivered with pain beneath me and I had to drop to my knees. I could have waited an entire age, in the mortal world, seas rising to consume the land and the sun parching the earth to nothingness. An eternity might have passed, beyond the seam of the real and the unreal.

I know you think I am a little girl, and what could a little girl know about eternity? But I do know this: whether you survive the ocean or you don't, whether you are lost or whether the waves deliver you back to shore—every story is told in the language of water, in tongues of salt and foam. And the sea, the sea, it whispers the secret of how all things end.

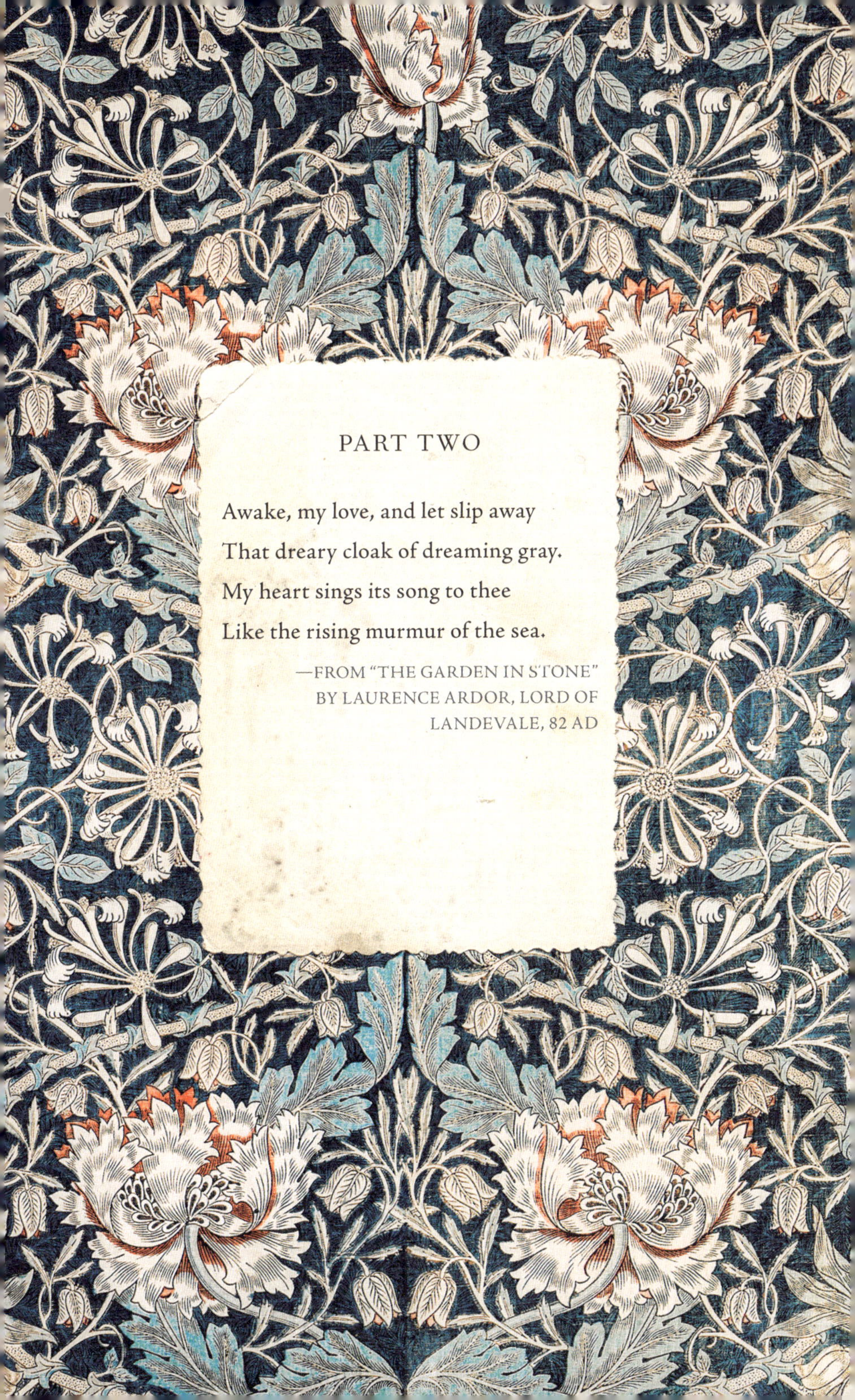

PART TWO

Awake, my love, and let slip away
That dreary cloak of dreaming gray.
My heart sings its song to thee
Like the rising murmur of the sea.

—FROM "THE GARDEN IN STONE"
BY LAURENCE ARDOR, LORD OF
LANDEVALE, 82 AD

THE UNIVERSITY OF LLYR

IN THE CITY OF CAER-ISEL

LITERATURE

FINE ARTS

ARCHITECTURE

HISTORY

MUSIC

How strange it is to live so long in the company of shadows that, without them, one feels bereft and needful of the dark.

The Llyrian Times

"The finest, printed."

Vol. CLXIV | Sixty-Eighth Day of Summer | Price: 1 Silver

UNIVERSITY STUDENTS TAKE AIM AT MYRDDIN'S LEGACY

Two undergraduate students from the University of Llyr have produced documents that, they claim, prove the authorship of Emrys Myrddin's beloved novel *Angharad* has been an elaborate, decades-long fabrication. The students allege that *Angharad* was really penned by Angharad Myrddin (née Blackmar), the late Myrddin's wife, and that Myrddin and others in his circle conspired to publish it under his name and pass it off as his own original work.

Angharad is a highly acclaimed artifact of Llyrian literary heritage, and Myrddin's recent interment in the Sleeper Museum reflects the magnitude of the novel's cultural impact. Originally published in 191, *Angharad* tells the story of a young woman seduced and held prisoner by the Fairy King, a beautiful but sinister chthonic deity. The novel boasts what literature professor and Myrddin scholar Cedric Gosse calls "universal appeal," and is celebrated both critically and commercially.

To bolster their claims about *Angharad*'s authorship, the undergraduate students have proffered a diary and a collection of letters, both purported to belong to Angharad Myrddin and which, they state, conclusively prove that Myrddin was not the novel's true author. Copies of the diary and these letters have been exclusively obtained by the *Times* and are currently under review by our editorial team. They will be vetted by our board, and, if their authenticity can be guaranteed, the *Times* has been given permission to release the documents publicly.

"The significance of these materials cannot be overstated," said Gosse, who leads the literature program at the University of Caer-Isel. "For the better part of a century Emrys Myrddin has been cloaked in a veil of secrecy and enigma. These letters not only provide insight into the circumstances surrounding *Angharad*'s writing and publication, but into the life and character of the man himself. I must say, I am awash with anticipation. This is the most exciting moment in my scholarly career."

Thomas Wetherell, the barrister for Myrddin's estate, declined to comment on the investigation. Angharad Myrddin herself also refused contact.

The *Times* reached out to her father, Colin Blackmar, author of "The Dreams of a Sleeping King" and one of Emrys Myrddin's close associates. He stated that these documents are "without a doubt forgeries" and that he would not hesitate to take legal action against the paper if they were published.

Kitteridge Marlowe, editor in chief of Greenebough Publishing, Myrddin's longtime publisher, echoed this sentiment.

"These claims are libelous and fraudulent," said Marlowe, in an incensed phone call, "and these students are nothing but opportunistic rabble-rousers. One of them is a woman, for Saints' sake, and the other is an Argantian."

The *Times* can confirm that one of these students is a woman—the first to be admitted to the university's prestigious literature college—and the other is an Argantian national.

As the twelve-year-long war with Argant continues with no end in sight, Myrddin's posthumously granted status as national author is seen by many to be essential in maintaining the potency of Llyr's army and the morale of its soldiers. In response to concerns about how these revelations might affect the war effort, Llyr's Ministry of Defense released a short missive:

"We trust that our colleagues at the Ministry of Culture are investigating these claims with rigorous scrutiny. In order to carry out such an investigation, however, the Ministry must be allowed to work discreetly and without interference and agitation from the public. When the truth behind these claims has been conclusively determined, the Ministry will decide upon a course of action."

The two students, Euphemia Sayre and Preston Héloury, could not be reached for comment.

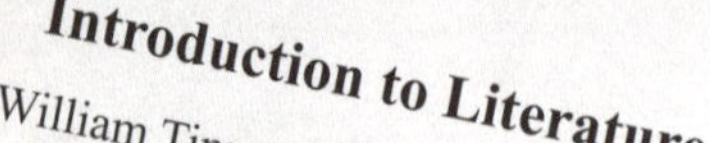

Introduction to Literature

Professor: Dr. William Tinmew

Class Meeting Time: MW 10:30 a.m.–12:00 p.m.

Class Location: Literature College, Theater 113

Office Hours: By appointment only—Literature College, room 304

Course Description: Introduction to Literature is a year-long course that offers students the opportunity to engage with the core texts of Llyrian literature. Students will be taught to properly annotate and to distinguish meter and rhyme and will learn fundamental skills that contribute to their capacity to think critically about works of literature.

Required Texts:

- "The Garden in Stone," by Laurence Ardor, Lord of Landevale
- *Artegall: A Romance*, by E. M. Inskip
- *A New Introduction to Formalism*, by Samuel Babbitt
- "Upon a Spring-Tide Storm I Rode," by Robin Crother
- *Exaltation to Caelia*, by A. E. Blount

All texts are available for purchase at the university bookstore.

When the glass with force was shattered
And the rose hue flew to your cheeks,
The flower petals blew and scattered,
And your lips parted, to speak.
You rose, at once, as if suspended,
A puppet on my own thin strings.
Your slumber, now, abruptly ended
The birds again began to sing.
Your eyes, they burned like twin torches;
Your lips were painted apple red.
Your gaze—I flinched, for how it scorches!
Were I infirm of spirit—oh, at once I might have fled!
But there I stood, in violet haze,
Still and frozen, heart astir,
I wished to feel the sun's stark rays.
How very sore and vexed you were!
When you spoke, your voice so hoarse,
I was pricked again by fear,
My blood ran frigid in its course,
And yet I strained and strained to hear.
"Though your chest is swelled with pride,
All that you see is not what it seems.
My form is rescued, but my soul has died,
For I found my deathless death in dreams."

This sets up the way that Angharad views him throughout the book—both a man and a monster by turns, corresponding with the way her husband can be both cruel and kind

And yet isn't this to my point? She is unable to separate her work from reality.

The way he came to me in my dreams, in my visions, was not quite how he appeared in the searing light of day. He seemed both more and less a man. Too pale to be mortal but more lively than a corpse. His hair was as dark and damp as a pour of water. The crown of bones showed the faintest of cracks; his veins were as blue as mine. Yet he was somehow more sinister for how he looked half a man. It was a skin he wore—I could tell as much at once. The mask that made me as keen to love him as I was to fear him.

again, the duality

or perhaps the madness?

[. . .]

He was Emrys, or the Fairy King—I no longer knew which—and he smiled at me. Beatifically, luxuriating in my rebellion, which was so petty to him that it was charming.

"I love you," he replied. "Why must you always resort to such base violence?"

"Because I do not have the power of eternity," I bit out.

He would laugh about this later, as he always did. "I am the one with the bruises," he would tell me jovially. "No one will believe your fables, darling girl. I appear the long-suffering husband."

[. . .]

The storyteller is a liar, but the story he tells is true.

cold
can't see
a thing.

That very first night—I can recall it well. A bridegroom, abed with his bride. But the Fairy King had some restraint, or perhaps he was delighting in the knowledge that he could have me, at any moment, and I could do nothing to protest. Circling me, as a wolf a wounded deer.

He lay beside me in silence, but he did not sleep. Could not, I don't think. What use has an immortal creature for slumber? What need an all-powerful being for the refuge of dreams? He was as cold as a stone in the sheets, both alive and dead at once.

I did not sleep, either. I did not know if I would ever sleep again. I shut my eyes and saw a star-pricked darkness. Miasmas of violet and searing green. I saw him, as he had come to me, pale and bony hand outstretched. His smile, all sharp teeth. His visage, so beautiful it could break a thousand hearts at once.

Much as I blinked and struggled against my own mind, I could not make these visions fade. Tears began to wet my face. And then the Fairy King turned, as though he could taste them in the air—and I broke into a girl's helpless sobs.

"My darling girl!" the Fairy King gasped as I shuddered and wept, flooding the tributaries made by the creases of our sheets with salt water. "Do not tremble—do not fear—let my touch chase away the covetous darkness of your dreams!"

But when he approached, he was Emrys the man—hair soaked and matted against his head, forearms laced with scratches, mud on his boots and the hem of his trousers. His white shirt was turned translucent with water. The fabric stuck to his chest, all its ridges and crevices that I knew so well, that I traced over with my hand in the dark.

"Come here," I whispered.

He did. Slowly, more water sliding off him with every step. The muscles in his throat pulsed.

"Please," I whispered again.

And then he sank down beside me on the chaise. At first he merely sat, still as stone, water spreading out in a stain around him, darkening the green velvet. And I—with as much shame as desire—fell forward onto him, exhaling short, tremulous sobs.

His arms came around me. His skin was cold, but underneath, when I felt the cords of muscle and heard the beat of his heart, I knew, in that moment, he was human. Or human enough.

He braced me against his chest. The movement was pure and simple, like an animal lowing to its mate. And when I squeezed my eyes shut, I saw nothing of the Fairy King, nothing of cruelty or captivity or hate.

All those years I cowered in the eternal night and yearned for the reprieve of day, but I had forgotten that the light has a certain cruelty of its own. One can shrivel on an arid shore as easily as one can drown in deep waters. I had become a creature of the dark, an ephemeral shade, ill-fit for the waking, sunlit world.

The Llyrian Times

"The finest, printed."

Vol. CLXIV | First Day of Fall | Price: 1 Silver

MASS DESERTION AT THE FRONT LINE PROMPTS NEW RECRUITMENT CAMPAIGN FROM THE MINISTRY OF DEFENSE, REPUDIATION OF RUMORS ABOUT MYRDDIN'S WORK

As a sudden cold front has blown in from Argant's mountains, carrying snow and freezing temperatures, so too has it appeared to carry something far more sinister: a wave of deserters, from Llyr's front line.

The Ministry of Defense circulated a report to its department—which the *Llyrian Times* has obtained exclusively from a whistleblower—detailing the extent of this desertion and its impact on the war effort. Generals from multiple legions claim that their numbers have dwindled almost overnight, and with each passing day the ranks seem to thin further. So as not to potentially undermine the war effort, our editorial board has decided to keep any additional details from this report confidential.

Minister of Defense Ellsworth Grindal responded to these rumors at a press conference on Tuesday.

"There is a reason that this report was meant only for the eyes of those within the Ministry," he said. "These are matters that ought to be treated with the utmost confidentiality, for the sake of national unity and patriotism. Should such rumors leak to our enemies, we may find the war effort—and the lives of our brave soldiers—at risk. I hope publications understand that this supersedes the importance of selling papers."

A Complete Biography of Laurence Ardor, Lord of Landevale

✤ Dr. Francis A. Rockflower ✤

The famed Laurence Ardor, future Lord of Landevale, was born Rhodri Morwent II, to a family of modest means in Marshsea. His father was a parish priest who was deeply committed to education, both religious and secular. The senior Rhodri Morwent used his church connections to secure his son a place at Locksley, a private secondary school which, at the time, only served children of Northern aristocratic extraction.

One might imagine that the young boy felt like an interloper within this affluent and opulent world, but he was quick to adapt to the social mores of the upper class and became popular with his schoolmates. By his third year, he had adopted the Northern name Laurence, and had also begun a relationship with Claribel Ardor, the beloved only daughter of the 1st Baron Landevale.

One might also imagine that an affair between individuals of such disparate backgrounds would be challenged and contested, but Laurence was well-loved by the baron, and he and Claribel were married with much joy and fanfare the week following Laurence's graduation.

Several years later, the baron took ill. From his deathbed, he named his son-in-law the new Lord of Landevale. Thus, one of Llyr's most celebrated and illustrious literary figures was born.

The first interred, a bard at the court of Llyr's earliest king. Aneurin is known for his incomplete and fragmentary epic the *Neiriad*, tracking the king Neirin's exploits and adventures, particularly his vanquishment of Argantian invaders. His virtue is power, and when he rises from his slumber, he will rekindle the spirit of victory won in this ancient war.

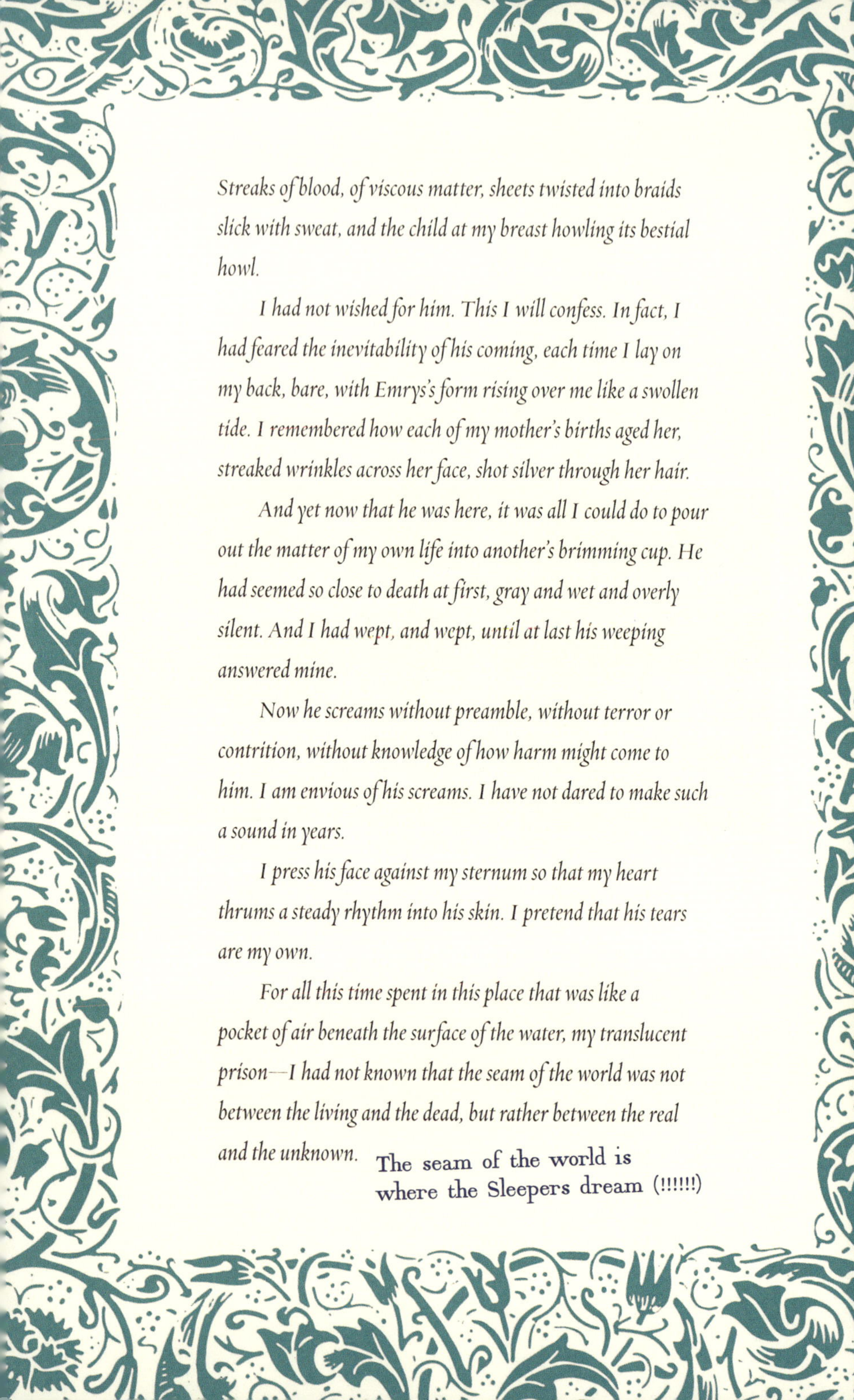

Streaks of blood, of viscous matter, sheets twisted into braids slick with sweat, and the child at my breast howling its bestial howl.

I had not wished for him. This I will confess. In fact, I had feared the inevitability of his coming, each time I lay on my back, bare, with Emrys's form rising over me like a swollen tide. I remembered how each of my mother's births aged her, streaked wrinkles across her face, shot silver through her hair.

And yet now that he was here, it was all I could do to pour out the matter of my own life into another's brimming cup. He had seemed so close to death at first, gray and wet and overly silent. And I had wept, and wept, until at last his weeping answered mine.

Now he screams without preamble, without terror or contrition, without knowledge of how harm might come to him. I am envious of his screams. I have not dared to make such a sound in years.

I press his face against my sternum so that my heart thrums a steady rhythm into his skin. I pretend that his tears are my own.

For all this time spent in this place that was like a pocket of air beneath the surface of the water, my translucent prison—I had not known that the seam of the world was not between the living and the dead, but rather between the real and the unknown.

The seam of the world is where the Sleepers dream (!!!!!!)

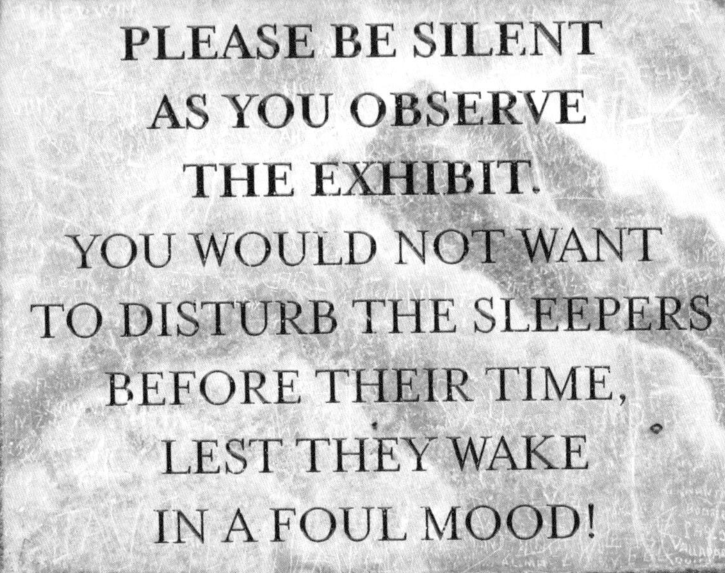
PLEASE BE SILENT
AS YOU OBSERVE
THE EXHIBIT.
YOU WOULD NOT WANT
TO DISTURB THE SLEEPERS
BEFORE THEIR TIME,
LEST THEY WAKE
IN A FOUL MOOD!

A Complete Biography of Laurence Ardor, Lord of Landevale

☙ Dr. Francis A. Rockflower ❧

There is arguably no force more significant in Laurence Ardor's life than love, be it romantic or familiar; whether for his wife, Claribel Ardor, or for the mysterious "Lady A," to whom many of Ardor's later works are addressed. Indeed, Ardor even wrote reverently of his father-in-law, the 1st Baron Landevale, to whom he owed a great debt—not only the transfer of his title and peerage, but the latter years of his informal education at the hands of the baron's private tutors.

Laurence Ardor's corpus could be said to be one magnificent and encompassing "letter of love" to those around him, or even an ode to the act of loving itself, in all its many forms. A romantic and a Romantic, Ardor's passionate manner of living is echoed in his poetry.

The most famous example is, of course, his seminal poem "The Garden in Stone," published in 82 AD. Composed following the death of his beloved wife, Claribel, it is widely considered one of the greatest works of Llyrian literature and earned Ardor his interment as a Sleeper. While "Garden" echoes the Romantic poetry of his contemporaries, it also draws from the themes, motifs, and symbols of the chivalric romances of his predecessors, such as Perceval ab-Owain. Ardor's "errant-knight" is a rendition of the typical protagonists of chivalric romances (purportedly directly inspired by ab-Owain's Corentin). This gives Ardor's work a surprising degree of intertextuality, enhancing its romanticism by calling on various influential literary traditions across time.

INTRODUCTION

The *Neiriad* is Llyr's foundational text. It is a heroic poem detailing the life and exploits of an ancient king, Neirin, and the most famous example from the tradition of epic poetry. Initially discovered in the first century BD, its authorship was unknown until the body of Aneurin the Bard was unearthed nearly a hundred years later. Aneurin's body, found slumbering in the remote hills of Southern Llyr, was accompanied by an incomplete—but undegraded—copy of the poem.

The *Neiriad*, composed in Old Llyrian, has been variously translated over the years, including a most well-known rendering by Tristram Marlais, commissioned by the nobleman Henry Windsor VI. This edition of the text is a revised version of Marlais's, which has updated the language for ease of reading.

The *Neiriad* begins somewhat unusually: not with the king's birth, but with his death. It is revealed, after the poem's first several stanzas, that the plot has in fact been the sleeping king's recollection. The battle that takes place is only a memory, recounted as Neirin slumbers in his tomb.

The curious nature of this opening has intrigued the literary field for centuries. Scholars have argued over its consequence and implications; writers have been moved by it to their art. (Colin Blackmar's "The Dreams of a Sleeping King" is a retelling of these iconic passages.) But academics and poets seem to agree unanimously on a single point: What is significant is not that the king sleeps but that he dreams.

A Complete Biography of Laurence Ardor, Lord of Landevale

✤ Dr. Francis A. Rockflower ✤

As the apocryphal tale goes, upon the death of his wife, Claribel, a weary-looking Ardor said to one of his servants, "Love whispers. Grief shouts."

The servant who related this story, Maud Raughley, is one of the most reliable sources for details about Ardor's life. Following Ardor's death, she was interviewed extensively by representatives from the Sleeper Museum for their pamphlets and biographies. Though a servant and a woman, she is noted for having her own rather poetic manner of speaking, and many of her direct quotes feature prominently in Sleeper-produced texts.

Maud was also a caretaker to Ardor's daughter, Antonia, especially following her mother's death. Though she often recounted stories about the young girl, few of those anecdotes have been compiled and maintained over the years. Antonia is not of great interest to scholars, and she herself passed away only a decade after her mother.

However, many of Maud's stories about Ardor hint at his relationship with Antonia: both loving and strained. A deeply passionate yet reclusive man, Ardor was reportedly protective of his daughter and dismissed several of her potential suitors. Antonia never married.

"Laurence despised the men who called," Maud said. "Perhaps he could not bear to see his daughter find a partner when he himself had lost his great love. He was a jealous creature. He did not even inter his wife's body until the smell began to come. Querulous, he was, like a swan that mates for life."

The third category of historic surnames from northern Argant includes concepts such as personal splendor and brilliance: power, dignity, eminence, veneration. From the old Argantian words *heluou* ("serious") and *ri* ("prince") comes the rare modern surname "Héloury."

Common surnames from this category are: "Catharan" (battle-iron), "Livirec" (great army), and "Kenan" (young warrior). These are all in the top twenty surnames in modern Argant. Below is a list of more unusual surnames (all below the top 10,000 in usage today):

Anhauer—"wealth-bold"
Bitimon—"daring-prince"
Fraval—"ardent-valorous"
Guinhael—"blessed-kinsman"
Haelon—"generous-prince"
Maduc—"godly"
Nimoe—"protector-prince"
Ruannel—"bright-lineage"
Sultiern—"sun-lord"
Tihern—"chieftain"
Yvain—"good-fire"

These names are most directly linked to Argant's age of heroes and represent an unbroken linguistic connection from the time of great kings to today.

SWEAR FEALTY
TO
NO CAUSE
BUT
KNOWLEDGE

the death of his beloved Claribel, Ardor became something of a recluse. He rarely left his bedroom and—owing to his blindness—required the near-constant attention of carers and housekeepers. This time of his life is not well-documented, but one of his maids, a woman by the name of Maud, reported that he kept the window beside his bed open at all hours, and in all temperatures.

Through the window he fingered the leaves of a nearby tree, and each morning when she came to give him his breakfast, he reported on the minute changes that had occurred to the tree overnight. The dying of leaves, the withering of branches by the encroaching winter winds.

"His world may have been small then," Maud said, "but it was not shallow."

One can imagine, then, why he would have been inspired to compose "The Garden in Stone," a work about a frozen, unchanging garden trapped in the sinister rigidity of time. Within the garden, the maiden sleeps and dreams, her mind at work even when her body is magicked to immortal stillness. And, of course, there is the gallant knight who comes to her rescue, ultimately freeing the maiden and her garden from this ill fate.

Composing this poem while blind was of course no mean feat, and Ardor employed an amanuensis to accomplish it. Historically, an amanuensis was often a slave or a servant; however, in Ardor's case, there is no record that any of his servants were literate. It is therefore generally agreed that his amanuensis was his own daughter, Antonia.

"I am seized by such love, I vow /
that I must come to ruin now."

The Caer Isel Post

TWELFTH DAY OF FALL

DEAN FOGG TAKING ORDERS FROM WEALTHY BENEFACTORS—WHO REALLY CONTROLS THE UNIVERSITY OF CAER-ISEL?

Lord Benedict Byron Southey, 8th Baron of Margetson, has been discovered pressuring Dean Fogg to institute conservative reforms at the university in exchange for a generous endowment. One of these proposed reforms is a university-wide pledge of loyalty, which all students will be instructed to sign, demonstrating their unflinching fealty to Llyr in the face of its ongoing war with Argant.

Whether the university will enact these reforms remains unclear, as both Dean Fogg and Baron Margetson have refused comment. The source of this information was an anonymous tip.

LETTERS
&
ANNALS

ANTONIA
ARDOR

The 22nd day of summer, 79 AD

Dear Diary,

I am thirteen today. A number of ill portent, I know, yet in spite of this, I am hopeful. Perhaps foolishly so. Clementina says that Grandfather's death has marked our family for further doom, and I came back from our tea crying, but Miss Maud told me that Clementina speaks in superstitions overheard from her parents, and has no wisdom herself. Then Miss Maud made me scones with clotted cream, though I felt too ill to eat.

But that was yesterday, when I was twelve. I am thirteen now and—Mother says—nearly a woman grown. I don't know if this is true, or what it means, if so. I still have my dolls and my velvet rabbit with buttons for eyes. I still have my book of fairy tales, which is falling apart for how much I have read it. I do so like the story of Ys. The city that fell. Father says I should read the Neiriad *(?) if I want the full tale, but when I tried to read the dusty old copy from his library, it made me tired. There are no mermaids in the* Neiriad.

For all this talk of being a woman now, Father still tucked me into bed last night. Perhaps it was the last time? I do like it when he reads to me, and there is a quote from the Neiriad *that has been stuck in my mind. "A king can reign a thousand years from a castle built in clouds." If only girlhood were such a kingdom. Nothing would ever change.*

Until next time, Diary
—A.A.

Such a blood-frenzy was the battlefield that the king—in
agitation—
Near turned his blade inside himself.
It was but for his most beloved ally,
That liege-man, who robed him in his armor,
Who raised for his king shield and sword,
Who spoke only plaudits and praise,
Who drank and ate only at his king's command.
The warrior-king called upon his liege-man,
Who retained his consciousness, and [. . .]
Brandished his war knife, battle-sharp,
*With the luster of [. . .] and love [*sic*] in his eyes.*
He halted the progression of the king's own blade,
Blood-slicked hand around blood-slicked hand
Voice hoarse from so many battle cries
With every breath the liege-man [. . .]
And thus, the battle halted, least in the king's mind,
*Still and suspended, as though in a dream [*sic*]*
There was some magic at work,
Nothing of the saints,
But the bitter malice of men made mythic,
And it infected the king, with the slickness of a fever
*This fever was love [*sic*] and it was [. . .]*
A great capacity had the king for this sentiment,
For his wife, who he held always in esteem,
And for his liege-man, who embraced him now,

*And for his country, its green hills and silver-blue [*sic*] waters*
It bore the scars of battle and the furrows of planting,
Yet it was a heavenly place, suffused with the [. . .] of a people
But this ruinous love, this poison,
Must be sweated out or torn by its roots
For it being more dangerous
To entertain sympathy with the Enemy
than to loathe them wholly . . .

Dearest Father,

perhaps you should consider not lying so baldly

I hope you will forgive the unexpected nature of this letter. You see, I have been so occupied with my studies that I've not had the chance recently to write to you. I have even been considering joining the university's polo team.

perhaps you should also consider not eluding the point

Are you well? Is the estate prospering in my absence? How is the hedge maze growing? Is my attendance sorely missed at your parties? I hope Mother is enjoying her trips to the opera. I hope that you are enjoying—as ever—your numismatics.

Through a regrettable lapse in judgment, I have provoked my professor into dismissing me from my seminar.

~~*There is perhaps the most infinitesimal of chances that I may have found myself in the unfortunate situation of being dismissed from my seminar.*~~ *Professor Damlet appears to harbor a grudge against me (perhaps he is one of those rascally forward-thinkers who resents the aristocracy?).* no

I'm most deeply sorry for causing this trouble and for disappointing you. I will do all I can to rise to your expectations in the future and to restore my standing with Professor Damlet. If you do happen to receive a letter from him, please disregard the part where he claims that I called him a twat. ~~*He has the tendency to embellish.*~~ let's just leave it at that, shall we?

Sincerely,

Your very favorite son, Lancelot

aren't you an only child?

LES CONTES DE FÉES D'ARGANT
ULYSSE GUÉGAN

INK IS THE BLOOD OF KINGS

THE

Literature College

AT THE

University of Caer-Isel

INVITES YOU TO ITS

Annual Midwinter Ball

ON THE EVE OF MIDWINTER

PLEASE COME IN YOUR FORMAL DRESS

THIS YEAR'S THEME IS

folklore

The 13th day of Winter, 80 AD

Dear Diary,

She is dead. My mother. Technically she has been dead for four days and sixteen hours now, if the physician is to be believed, if I am calculating exactly from the moment she drew her final breath.

Though four days have passed—both too quickly and also as slow as a drip of honey from a spoon—she has not been buried yet. Father refuses. He says we must wait until the sculptor fashions her death mask, but I suspect he simply cannot bear to part with her body, when he knows he will never see her again. She will be interred in the Ardor mausoleum with Grandfather, in the field where the asphodel and infant's breath bloom. The crypt is white marble, such that it is almost camouflaged amidst all those ivory blooms. And due to the shelter of a flowering pear tree, the petals are arranged neat and uncommonly still. Even in such bitter winds, the daisies never blow.

In this garden of stone, someday I will be laid to rest, too. Miss Maud tells me not to think of it, but how can I not? The only inevitability of our existence is death. I wish I did not carry this knowledge at only age fourteen. I can only imagine that it will get heavier and heavier as I grow old.

Until next time, Diary
—A.A.

It has occurred to me that I don't quite know the same kind of grief as Antonia. My mother and even my grandparents still live. And my father—I never met him. He's not even a ghost to me. So how can I grieve him?

But Preston grieves his. He knew his father, loved him, and watched him fade to a shadow. He doesn't speak of him often, but whenever he does, the memory impresses itself on me. I feel as if I know him, a little bit. A sharply clever if rather quiet man, a master of chess and puzzles, a lover of animals, even the smallest rabbits. I can easily see how I might have loved him, and I hope he would have loved me, too.

Already I love so many of his pieces, the pieces in Preston: his cleverness, his patience, his slight aloofness that I adore as much as it frustrates me. I know he wears his father's watch, even with its worn leather band.

But the more I love him, the more I'm afraid of losing him. Even now I don't understand why he chose me. With my bad head, my skittishness, my flightiness. All the shadows I can still see in the corners of the room. I'll never be free of them, not really. And so maybe I'll always be looking for that escape hatch, that hole in the floor.

Except for those few peaceful moments in bed beside him. When he's holding me and when reality is better than anything I might dream.

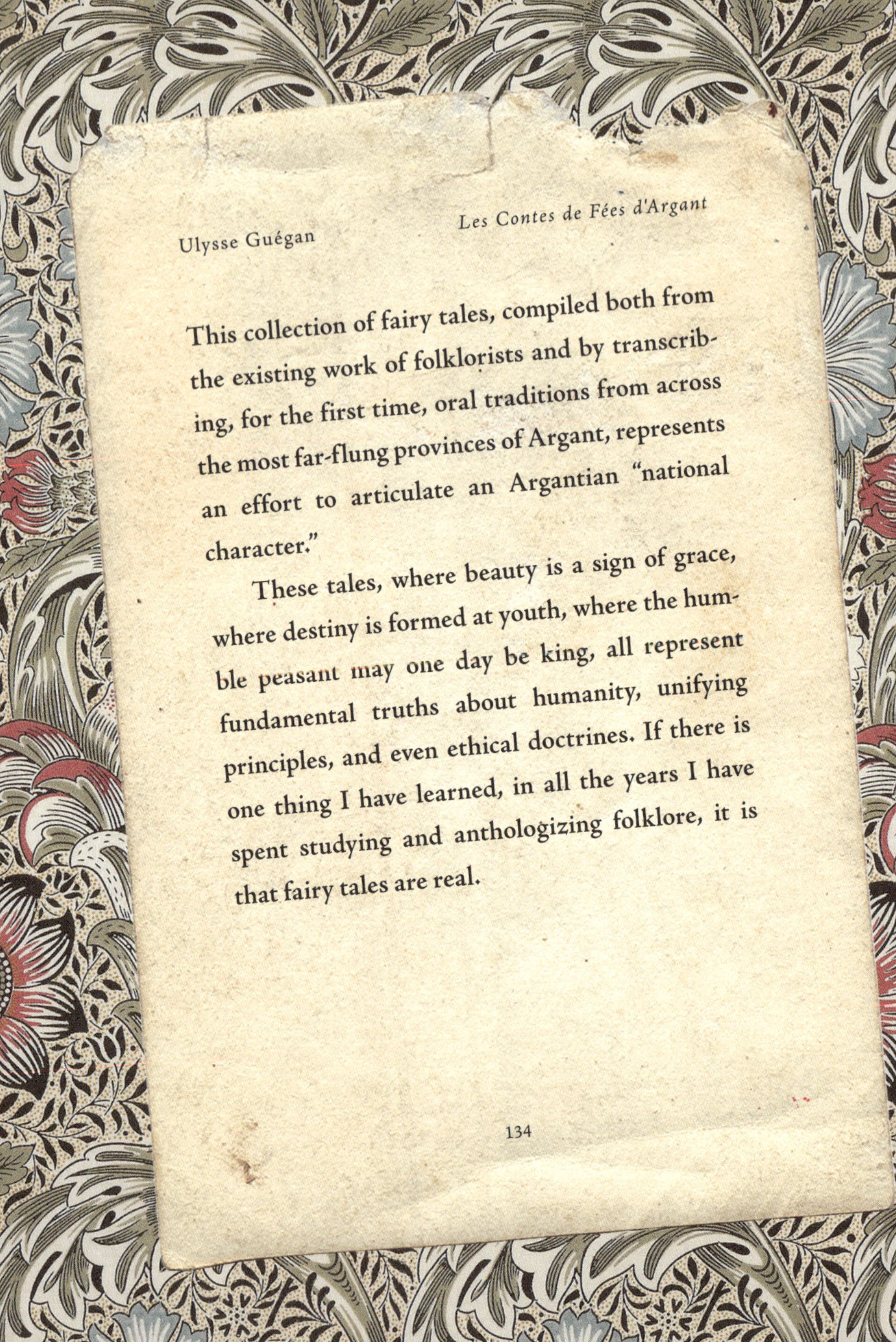

This collection of fairy tales, compiled both from the existing work of folklorists and by transcribing, for the first time, oral traditions from across the most far-flung provinces of Argant, represents an effort to articulate an Argantian "national character."

These tales, where beauty is a sign of grace, where destiny is formed at youth, where the humble peasant may one day be king, all represent fundamental truths about humanity, unifying principles, and even ethical doctrines. If there is one thing I have learned, in all the years I have spent studying and anthologizing folklore, it is that fairy tales are real.

There was a king who reigned in the age of old, and he was known as a great king, a king for all the island, beloved and wise. He built a grand city of marble and stone. His city bustled with artisans and craftsmen, with bards and poets. It was called the city of Ys. He brought silver from the North and gold from the South to adorn himself and his only daughter, Dahut.

The king was a widower, and so he loved his daughter as well as he had once loved his wife. But Dahut was young and spirited and not always mindful of her duty. She often wandered from her tower in the king's glorious castle, the tower that rang sonorously with the city's bells. And during one of these wanderings, she encountered a handsome youth.

The youth loved her at once for her beauty, and she at once loved the youth for his graces and the dreams he put in her head of adventure and freedom. Dahut and the youth began to meet secretly at night, in only the silvery gleam of the moon. He swore he would keep faith with her always, and she swore in turn that she would renounce her crown and her title and live with him as a common maiden, not a princess.

But Dahut knew her father would never relinquish her, and, imprisoned in that gray tower, her days were ill and her nights worse. Her father came and went from her chamber as he pleased. And so, one evening, Dahut stole her father's silver key and plotted her escape.

The youth came to the castle to aid her, but the king's men caught him. He was dragged to the throne room, where he confessed all. Dahut was forced to watch as her father killed her life's great love, and her screams could be heard through every corridor of the castle, her sobs for the dreams that had been stolen.

The king reached out, to take hold of his daughter's hand and drag her back to the tower. But Dahut had now tasted true passion and pure love and would not be imprisoned again. From the king's belt she wrestled his sword, and she cut off her own father's hand to free herself from his grasp.

Distraught by the loss of her lover, Dahut fled the castle and dove into the ocean. The saints took pity on her and, rather than let her drown, transformed her into a mermaid. The king was fitted with a silver hand but, so aggrieved by the loss of his daughter, he never lifted a sword again. Indeed, he rarely left his chambers, and the great city of Ys began to wilt and decay, as a flower garden left dry and unattended.

In retaliation for the king's cruelty and apathy, it is said that the sea itself rose up and swallowed the city. The great stone cracked, and the artisans and bards were drowned.

But all was not lost when the city of Ys sank beneath the waves. Under the sea, mermaids pray in the cathedral. Under the sea, fire burns green. Under the sea, its great bells still toll. And it is said that the city may one day rise again, lifting from its ocean tomb, and whoever first hears the music of the bells will be its new king.

Perhaps this revelation will seem overly simple to you—like a child's discovery, not a grown woman's. But my girlhood was stolen from me, so how am I to know better?

What made it perhaps most difficult is that he was not always a monster. His kindness seemed to come as easily as his cruelty. He could strike me one moment and then bandage the very wounds he had inflicted, hold me against him while I sobbed. The monster inside him twisted like a serpent, showing by turns its belly and then its teeth.

Eventually, I forgot even weeping. I became so obscure to myself, my mind so severed from my physical form, that I could persuade no tears to fall. The grief was a silent blade, and it scraped me clean. I would have welcomed tears—truly. They would have reminded me that I was still alive. Despite it all. I was glad for every kick of the child within me, even though it hurt—perhaps especially when it hurt. Only a living creature can cringe in pain.

My revelation, as I lay on the green chaise in the office, facing the window that showed only a square of cold gray sky, was this: The man who I thought had saved me was in truth the one who had caged me. With that epiphany, I drifted and was lost. There is no bleaker darkness than that found when the light of love is snuffed out.

The Llyrian Times

"The finest, printed."

Vol. CLXIV | Fourth Day of Winter | Price: 1 Silver

AS WAR WITH ARGANT INTENSIFIES, LLYRIAN GOVERNMENT ORDERS RESTRICTIONS ON CULTURAL ACTIVITIES

Last week, as the Llyrian army launched a new offensive that aims to breach the border with Argant, the Ministry of Defense and the Ministry of Culture released a joint statement announcing a nationwide restriction on all activities that could be seen as dissident. This includes a curtailment of certain publications, including this newspaper's planned exposé on Emrys Myrddin.

At the beginning of winter, two students from the University of Caer-Isel contacted the paper with documents that, they claim, prove that Emrys Myrddin is not the author of the seminal novel *Angharad* and possibly other work attributed to him. Our editorial board has vetted these materials carefully and initially planned to publish the findings by the end of the year; however, this new measure by the government has delayed our article indefinitely.

Emrys Myrddin is the seventh Sleeper of Llyr, interred at the museum only this past year following his death. His consecration was widely viewed as a boon to Llyr's war effort, providing the army with a much-needed boost in morale, and—if the government and the more superstitious among us are to be believed—bestowing Llyr with a boon of magic.

But the recent controversy has cast a pall over the nation, allegedly weakening this enchantment and enervating morale at a time when, according to the missives from the Ministries of Culture and Defense, "it can hardly be afforded." The newspaper reached out to the office of the culture minister, Stuart Skirclaw, for further comment.

"This is the moment for the nation of Llyr to unite in common cause," Minister Skirclaw said. "It is of grave importance to conclude this war as quickly as possible, with as few casualties as possible on either side, and this temporary ban on seditious activities is intended to minimize the cost of this prolonged conflict. Indeed, the sooner Argant surrenders, the sooner full civil liberties will be restored."

When asked whether the

missive was specifically targeting the press, Minister Skirclaw replied, "Naturally, some cultural institutions will be more affected by these restrictions than others. Our ministry understands and acknowledges that newspapers will bear the brunt. However, we ask that you hold tight for the sake of your fellow countrymen and pray for an expeditious end to this war."

The *Times* and other newspapers are not the only institutions that have been forced to make swift adjustments. At the University of Caer-Isel, a number of classes have been canceled for being "detrimental to the spirit of national unity," and others have had their coursework modified to ensure "conformity with the new restrictions and unflagging loyalty to the government and the war effort."

The *Times* reached out to the university's dean, Quincy Fogg, but his office did not respond to our request for comment.

Other measures that have been implemented at the university include a ban on correspondence; the porters' lodges have reportedly been told to stop accepting post marked for Argant and to turn away any mail coming from the enemy nation. The *Times* spoke to one university student, Domenic Byron Southey, the son of the 8th Baron Margetson, who said that these measures are "long past due."

"The university has fostered an overly permissive environment where sedition has festered among its student body," Southey said. "Hopefully with these restrictions we will see these traitorous elements silenced."

I have been completely captivated by Antonia's letters lately, unfortunately to the detriment of my other work. But there is so much within them that resonates with me. I haven't felt such a spark with any of my other course readings. (How would anyone's soul be set alight by formalism??)

In her letters, Antonia writes to her oldest and dearest friend, Clementina. Despite the fact that they are separated, their friendship perseveres. It's rather beautiful to me. Even though Antonia expresses her pain, she is able to do so very eloquently. Grief doesn't erase her personhood; it doesn't erode her intelligence, her wit, her mind. She is such a real and full person that she seems to lift off the page. I'm almost able to picture her, in my room with me.

It feels almost like reading "Angharad"—or at least, how it used to. That book is different now. Not worse, but harder. I see all its sharp edges. And I can certainly see the sharp edges of Antonia's letters, too. Her pain cuts through time. Yet, in the strangest sense, it heals me as much as it hurts me.

We are separated by so many years, but I know her. She feels like a friend, the way that Angharad did. Maybe it really is as simple as that. The words make her real. It's been a long time since this epiphany occurred to me, in all of its wonderful straightforwardness. The power of writing. The reason I want to study literature at all.

In Defiance of Death, and of Genre: the *Neiriad* as a Romance

by Dr. Morgan Malory

With such a significant work as the *Neiriad*, it is nearly impossible for there to be a predominant interpretation, though some theories have certainly been more mainstream than others. This paper will discuss the various prevailing theories, not merely weighing their validity but contextualizing them in the times and places in which they became prevalent.

For example, the readings of the *Neiriad* that focus on the relationship between Neirin and his favored companion—and its various homoerotic implications—were most fashionable in the era referred to as "literary heresy," when it became popular to assign subversive meaning to Llyr's foundational texts. Though no longer in vogue, such trends demonstrate that the academic, social, and economic milieu exerts enormous influence over the work of scholars of the *Neiriad*.

We may look at another moment in time, equally exemplary if rather less subversive, which has in fact grown in popularity in recent years. There is a small but influential contingent of scholars whose work has heavily focused on the relationship between Neirin's daughter and her lover in the *Neiriad*. This narrative arc, they insist, exemplifies the core themes of Aneurin's epic and is more salient than the tales of Neirin's military exploits.

Their scholarship argues that the *Neiriad* is, in fact, not a war story but a love story. That it ends tragically is often the sticking point, as most literature considers a happy ending to be fundamental in defining a romance.

Can one still cherish a love that ends in grief?

Dearest Clementina,

The one benefit to my isolation is that it has given me much time, and much cause, to reminisce about our happiest moments. Do you recall, too, how we stripped down to our shifts and waded into the river, water crisp and cool against the oppressive summer air? Do you remember that we frolicked barefoot in the grass, weaving daisy chains and placing them in our hair? These are some of the happiest moments of my life, and I will love you, always, for painting my memory in such bright hues.

Best of all, perhaps, I remember our secret visits to my father's library, how we carefully—though gleefully—pulled those old tomes down from his shelves, surreptitiously cracking the leather spines. I relish the recollection of these rebellious moments. Girlhood dressed us in fearlessness. We were reckless in our innocence.

We read fairy stories and dreamed of those knights in shining armor. Brave, loyal, clever, and good. They littered the earth with the corpses of slain dragons and climbed the ivy to reach us in our secret towers.

Now, in my advanced age, I have begun to wonder what lies beneath the helmet and mail. These knights—are they rageful? Are they callous? Or worse—are they simply mortal, given to all the passions and tempers of ordinary men? I find such a thought so difficult to bear. Would that I could still believe in the untarnished gold of our girlhood heroes.

MYTHS AND LEGENDS OF SOUTHERN LLYR

Perceval Haldane

The stories of the peasants of Southern Llyr have long been dismissed as rambling superstitions; it is only in recent decades that folklorists have begun to consider them as academic subjects. There is much to be learned from these tales, not merely ethnography or anthropology, but even about the history of Llyr itself. After all, without these stories, researchers would never have come upon perhaps the greatest vestige of Llyrian history, a legend made manifest.

The sleeping body of Aneurin the Bard was discovered in the second century BD, beneath a green knoll in the most remote hills of Southern Llyr. But, according to the Southern Llyrians of the area, this was no secret—they knew, all along, that the king's bard was asleep under the hill. They simply also knew not to disturb him.

Indeed, these peasants all bore a consistent tale: that, if one were to encounter a fairy in the woods or on the moors, the fairy would ask the question: "Does Aneurin the Bard still live?"

The only way to keep from being killed or ferried away to the realm of the fae was to reply, "For now, he sleeps, but he will wake again, to reign and conquer the world." Then the fairy would allow you to pass unharmed.

The Old King, Neirin, repels the "silver-clad" Enemy who speaks Ankou's tongue (Argantians)

His Daughter (nameless) is seduced by the Enemy into betraying the King, which causes his city to fall beneath the waves

"Les Contes de Fées d'Argant"—contains a similar story, only the daughter is given a name and portrayed in a more sympathetic light

The sins of the king are instead blamed for the fall of the city of Ys / Ker-Is / Caer-Isel

He is fitted with a hand of silver

Of silver

Of silver

Young unbeliever, your mind as sharp as steel;

it is for you and only you that the great bells peal.

What became of the mermaid Dahut? Was she caught in some sailor's net and carried to shore as his unwilling bride like a selkie stripped of its skin? Did she wash up on the dry-cracked shore and die of thirst, the water just a finger's reach away? Or did she remain beneath the waves, in a palace of alabaster coral, a labyrinth of her own design, never again straining for the light of the sun? Mermaids can breathe water as mortals breathe air, but all living creatures can drown.

I have begun to feel a certain passion rise in me as well, though it is a tangled and winding thing, sometimes perverse. I am helping to create something that I believe—truly—will be a great work of art, which will reverberate beyond the years of my life and into eternity.

Nothing is ever lost, only changed, and grief is no more than the knowledge that a wilted flower cannot be made again to bloom. I am not truly so puffed with pride that I believe my work will shift the order of the world, but I do believe that it may do that perhaps for one person. One girl, who finds herself in the same garden as I am, in white flowers, in a coffin of glass. Will she see me, through these words, as if peering through a dusty window? I allow myself to hope. To dream.

WAYWARD DAUGHTER: A MELODY FOR DAHUT

by Rhiannon Beddoe

Do you think she ever prayed,
That wayward daughter, doomed to fall?
If she had believed, would it matter?
Would her story have been so small?
We have tales of saints,
And tales of kings
And knights who wield their swords
But what tales are there for wayward girls,
What melodies, what chords?
Girls are born to regret,
To kneel and to be little mourned
Even a princess, so renowned
Is just the same as the wife low-born,
The miller's daughter, the scullery maid
And every woman dead and gone
She was as much a future queen
As she was a pawn
She was like a mermaid for her beauty,
And kind and just and good;
But all such virtues pale against
The would and could and should.
Now we say with puffed-up pride,
And none of Dahut's pain
She could have stayed,
She would have reigned,
She never should have loved.

Lo! How we have heard the deeds and glory
Of the last and greatest king;
How he broke the land through sea
As quick as the spear shafts of his enemies;
How he kept at bay the water
Just as he repelled the pillagers
Who threatened his supremacy
Famed raiser of both sword and cup,
The king was as beloved by his men
As loathed by his enemies
He drank deeply of his mead,
And of his own repute,
Yet never for a moment
Was he forgetful of his company
In the flower of his war-fame
The king thought to further honor his men
And by glory in battle, no man would refuse
This call to arms and offer of blessings
Even the saints could not sway them
From sharpening their blades
From girding their bodies, and whetting their enmity
Much bitter blood was spilled,
All for cause of man's caprice
And ill-fated seeking of legacy.

The Scribe Review: A New Journal for Creative Nonfiction

The Prophecy
by Taylor Cardew

Our stories are all the same. We dream a common dream. There is but one tale, though it spreads itself like the branches of an oak, taking on knots and whorls. It is told in many tongues, in many voices, across all of space and time. It strains and strains through the ages. And if we ever think we can escape it, we find ourselves within it once more, turning in its endless labyrinth.

Not all of it is grief. Love, this most strident tale, endures. And indeed, there are versions of the story where you save her. You climb the ivy to her tower and she follows you down again—neither of you looks back. When the waves drag at you and the storm beats down, you keep hold of her hand. You escape the flooding city moments before it crumbles into the sea. You kiss her and she wakes. You find a horse, a carriage, a ship, or even just a hatch in the floor.

But the versions where you lose her are the oldest stories in the world. The ones where you fall, where you drown, where you let go of her hand. Where you kiss her but she remains as cold and still as stone. There are no horses or carriages or ships to bear you away. There is no hatch in the floor.

Always I had been a creature of much carousing, given to dancing barefoot in the grass, laughing too loudly and gaily, in some manner more body than mind. (Are all children not alike in this manner?) Yet now I began sleeping for days at a time. I had lost that girlhood glee, that easy joy, the wildness that moved my form.

When my husband rose, I remained in bed, not even lifting my cheek from the pillows. My hair knotted and tangled in the sheets. Never before had it been so easy for me to succumb to the darkness and oblivion of slumber. More often than not, he was happy to leave me undisturbed. So long as I was in our bed, I was sufficiently contained.

Yet my mind, unlatched from my body, escaped him in ways he could not see.

There is only so much any mind can endure before it must reject reality. Before it must reject wisdom and reason. I have always found my fragments of freedom in fantasy. It has served me better than any shield or sword, and certainly better than any of the laws of men. I have lived and died by quill and ink. And how could I ever begrudge myself this? Even moths and cormorants are thought by the naturalists to dream. I may have been a girl when he came for me, but I am most assuredly a woman now. I had thought I might grow strength in my years, as an elm thickens and spreads its roots, but I feel in many respects weaker than I ever was before. If there is one great virtue of girlhood, it is the insulation of dreams.

We are protected, as children, by our belief in the unreal. In moments of solitude I can turn back time and imagine myself as young again: my bare feet in the grass, a crown of white flowers and juniper berries in my hair. I can make myself believe in knights and heroes, in such sweet-voiced and pure-hearted saviors.

I take refuge in these dreams. I dive eagerly into unreal waters. But when I return, dragged unwillingly to the shore like a mermaid in a net, I am bereft again. Womanhood has left me with no place to hide.

My body will be as
still as those in their
glass mausoleums, but
my mind will be so
alive as to rend the
world apart.

When upon your pallid cheek
The purple twilight lay,
I came, an errant-knight oblique,
To trespass the gray arch-way.
The mists of dusk were in the air,
A murmur in the willow trees,
And should it PLEASE the maiden fair,
The rust-checked latch sprang FREE.
Upon her bed of flowers and vines,
In her grave of glass,
The maiden slept, an idol in its shrine,
No more a gay and larking lass.
The errant-knight cut through the thorns,
And knelt, as if to mourn.
Both a HERETIC and a supplicant,
Struck as much by love as he was by SCORN.
All precious things shatter, if they are found too soon.
I, in my brusque armor, was indeed afeared,
For like a piece of glass you were, so very finely hewn.
So with a slowness quite like agony, I was quiet as I neared.
The blood remains within your veins,
Your lashes pale upon your cheeks,
As dead wheat on the plain.
Yet though you breathe, you cannot speak
With a swell of grief, I make to raise my blade.
My own blood roared and clashed, not unlike a storm

How sad it is, to see a maid
So shackled to her form!
I could not hope to break the glass
By such brute mortal means
I knelt instead upon the grass,
And from my throat, a grief-struck keen.
[. . .]
Here the darkness, there the light,
Here the lady and her knight.
As petals scatter out to sea,
Their tale folds into eternity.

I have been long at work on the task at hand; longer still have I pondered the true purpose of it. We are not an inordinately unhappy nation, at least that I can see, though the limits of my position perhaps prevent me from perceiving the grueling indignities and daily turmoil of, say, a peasant in his sinking hovel. They who know as much of the lives of kings and heroes as a flea knows of the Saints' liturgies—perplexingly I am told that it is them who I write for, they who cannot even read.

I think I have been misled in this matter. Those who style themselves kings are the ones who require reassurance of a king's inviolability, of his immortality. The aristocrats in their wigs, the princes in their palaces—all the virtues and blessings of mortal life they have attained, and yet still they are so afraid.

I write to reassure them of their own immortality. They are all little men, in truth, frightened of death and more so of insignificance, no different from the peasants they scorn. They are afraid to accept that a king can die. They are afraid to accept that, in the end, all kings must.

Nothing remained of him, not even that coronet of bone. Not even a strand of black hair, carried aloft on the salty breeze. Yet the brine I tasted was not the air; it was my own tears, wetting my face, falling to my lips. Blood, tears, seawater—all of it salt.

My grief was a strangely faceted thing. It showed a different face when I turned it over and over again in my mind. The tears dampened the golden hair that spread about me on the floor. It was darkened, tarnished. The shining golden hue of girlhood was gone. I mourned it, as fiercely as I mourned my husband, as fiercely as I had hated him and loved him. The parts of me that he had made were indistinguishable from those he had not.

He raised me up high and put a crown on my head, and thus when he crumbled, so did I. My fall from heaven hurt more than all my days of living hell. But lying there, my ribs cracked, the ashen remains of the Fairy King scattered around me like blown wheat, I drew my first true breath in decades. Every inhale ached. And yet that was how I knew I was alive. How I knew I was free.

Her grief is her release.
It is her freedom.
I understand now.

The Llyrian Times

"The finest, printed."

VOL. CLXIV | Twelfth Day of Winter | Price: 1 Silver

SLEEPER MUSEUM DESTROYED IN FREAK ACCIDENT

On Tuesday evening, an unexpected and devastating tragedy befell Llyr's beloved Sleeper Museum, when, without warning, the building crumbled and then sank into the waters of Lake Bala.

The museum was closed at the time and no staff or security were on the premises, so no injuries or casualties have been reported. However, the museum itself has been utterly destroyed. There seems to be no explanation for this sudden collapse, and when our editorial team spoke with Bastien & Lewis, the architectural firm that designed the building, they were adamant that it could not be due to any structural defects.

"The Sleeper Museum is our firm's greatest achievement," Benedict Crother, a spokesperson for Bastien & Lewis, stated. "We are confident there is no design flaw that could have caused this tragic incident. The current leaseholder is responsible for the building's upkeep."

"The museum was examined last spring and was up to code in all areas," said Roderick Somervell, the museum's curator. "Nothing had fallen into disrepair."

Our reporters also reached out to a team of naturalists at the School of Practical Studies, to investigate whether or not there could be a climatological explanation for the occurrence. They suggested that perhaps the unseemly winter weather had weakened the structure of the building or that the recent large accumulations of snow put undue pressure on the foundation. However, they were puzzled by the suddenness of the occurrence.

"If this terrible tragedy is due to environmental factors, it certainly would not have happened all at once," said Dr. Alby Crane, the leader of the team. "There would have been significant damage—cracks in the stone—to foretell the building's destruction. Unless, of course, there were warning signs that were missed by the museum staff."

Somervell is insistent that there were no such warning signs. "I have been in charge of this museum for over a decade," he stated. "It has prevailed and flourished under my care." When asked for his guess as to how this incident occurred, Somervell replied simply, "The only explanation is either foul play or magic."

As for the accusation of foul play, Somervell refused to elaborate, stating only that "we all know Llyr's true enemy." This sentiment has been echoed by a number of citizens—in a flash poll, 62 percent of respondents stated that this was the result of an Argantian plot to destroy Llyr's most celebrated and hallowed landmark.

But there is no evidence of this assertion, nor any suggestion as to how an alleged act of intentional destruction would have been committed, given that the Llyrian-Argantian border has been closed for months. It seems the only remaining explanation—which can be neither proven nor disproven—is that which Somervell himself proposed: magic.

A king can reign a thousand years from a castle built on clouds.
[. . .]
The swirling surf shielded the king's death,
His body buried in its salt grave, the tide to pick his bones—
For so great a man, he was made small in his ending,
Small as any peasant, low as any serf.
He had no song to sing, no [. . .] to behold.
*It was only his daughter, lonely Dahut [*sic*], who trilled on,*
*In the swell of the Sea [*sic*],*
Yearning still for her lost lover.
Her song was love, and it was eternal.

The Llyrian Times

"The finest, printed."

Price: 1 Silver

Fifteenth Day of Winter

Vol. CLXIV

LLYRIAN GROUND OFFENSIVE FALTERS—MORALE DROPS AMONG INFANTRY AS NEWS OF SLEEPER MUSEUM DESTRUCTION REACHES FRONT LINE—AFTER UNEXPECTED LOSSES, DISCUSSIONS OF ARMISTICE RENEWED

This Ticket entitles
Effy Sayre
to a Sight of the
SLEEPER MUSEUM
at the Hour of ten on
Wednesday the second of spring, 237 AD

Let no one say that I am weak.

I am fearful, and therefore brave.

I am wounded, yet all the stronger for it.

The Llyrian Times

"The finest, printed."

Vol. CLXIV | First Day of Spring | Price: 1 Silver

PEACE TREATY SIGNED, ENDING TWELVE YEARS OF WAR BETWEEN LLYR AND ARGANT

As of this morning, a peace treaty has been officially signed by dignitaries from the governments of Llyr and Argant, putting an end to the twelve-year-long war between the nations. The full text and provisions of the treaty have not yet been made public; however, the *Llyrian Times* has learned exclusively that it includes a restoration of the border to its 196 lines, an easing of sanctions, and a reinstitution of diplomatic relations. The Llyrian government has also agreed to pay the government of Argant an unspecified amount to aid in the reconstruction of civilian areas that were damaged in the conflict.

This treaty comes after unexpected and heavy losses to the Llyrian side in a recent skirmish, during which the Llyrian army was forced into a temporary surrender. Prior to this battle at Four Crosses (in Argantian, Quatre-Croix), Llyr's military leaders projected confidence, leading many to believe that victory was assured and would be definite, perhaps even ending the war in Llyr's favor.

The crushing defeat—and the subsequent armistice—has left the nation reeling. It has long been accepted that Llyr's army is superior, with greater stores of wealth from which to draw and state-of-the-art military technology that outclasses that of Argant. By contrast, Argant has often relied on irregular tactics, such as ambushes and surreptitious attacks on supply lines.

None of these tactics were on display in the Battle of Four Crosses, however. The Argantian and Llyrian armies met in open field. Thus far there has been no official statement on the cause of Llyr's hasty and conclusive defeat; however, morose speculation hangs in the air. The timing is all too convenient to ignore: the Battle of Four Crosses took place a mere day after the sudden, devastating destruction of Llyr's Sleeper Museum.

The more superstitious citizens of Llyr will say that our nation has lost something far more essential than the war. Indeed, while tanks can be refurbished and army ranks replenished, there is no easy remedy for the ruination of faith. The Llyr that emerges from this war will be unquestionably changed. It remains to be seen how, exactly, our nation restores its sense of self. What will be the new foundation of our country's character? Who will be our heroes now?

ANNOUNCING THE ANTONIA ARDOR MEMORIAL ENDOWMENT

The esteemed literature college at the University of Llyr is pleased to share that it will now be endowing a scholarship for the study of the writings of female authors. The first of its kind, this endowment was funded by Angharad Myrddin and the Myrddin and Blackmar estates.

Beginning in the next academic year, a panel of professors from the literature college, as well as Mrs. Myrddin herself, will select an incoming student to receive this scholarship, which will cover the full costs of university attendance. The selected student will also receive dedicated mentorship from professors at the literature department, to encourage their academic growth.

Please submit a cover letter with all relevant biographical and academic information and an essay of approximately 2,000 words, explaining your interest in this topic and how you will contribute to the field with your scholarship. You may use the scholarship's first paper, Euphemia Sayre's "The Ethics of Amanuensis," as a guide. The deadline for the application is no later than the first day of spring.

We look forward to reading your materials and welcoming an eager and dedicated new student to the literature college.

The Ethics of Amanuensis: A Case Study Concerning "The Garden in Stone"

by EUPHEMIA SAYRE

ABSTRACT: "The Garden in Stone," the acclaimed poem by Laurence Ardor, Lord of Landevale, is widely touted as his consummate work and almost single-handedly established his status as one of Llyr's seven Sleepers. Despite the typicality of the formalist approach in reading "Garden," taking into account the biographical details surrounding the poem's composition offers a novel analysis of its style and themes. This paper argues that Ardor's use of an amanuensis—his daughter, Antonia—contributed significantly to "Garden's" content and must be considered in any serious scholarship. It also proposes that the use of an amanuensis presents its own ethical dilemmas for both the poem's academic study and its popular reception.

For the final time, with the Fairy King's ashes still clinging to my gown, I made my way to the water. It was dusk, and the tide pools were alight, limpid gold like coins tossed into a fountain. I could have made a hundred wishes.

Instead, I lowered myself onto the sand, kneeling precisely where the tide-foam lipped the shore. It washed the hem of my gown, tugging it gently and turning it as translucent as a bridal veil. I recall being shocked that my mind would supply such a comparison. I wore no such garment when I was wed to the Fairy King. He had no desire to observe mortal rites. And yet his lips, against mine, were both as soft and as wanting as any man's.

Only in his final moments would he have known that. When he realized, as his flesh withered on his bones, that he, too, could perish as banally as the mortals he reviled.

I rose then, lifting my damp gown, and waded into the sea until I was drowned to the knees. A sudden, wild joy overtook me. I laughed, a raucous and girlish sound. It arced out over the water like a skimming tern.

If you can learn to love that which despises you, that which terrifies you, you can dance on the shore and play in the waves again, like you did when you were young. Before the ocean is friend or foe, it simply is. And so are you.

Just now I have begun to dream the strangest dreams, the visions from which follow me even through my waking hours. They are not unpleasant dreams—no, far from it. In these fantasies, I "wake" inside a coffin of glass. This may seem a frightful occurrence, but my heart and mind are absent of fear.

When I open my eyes, the glass shatters and vanishes. I rise. I am in a grand hall of statues and I can taste the brine of seawater in the air. The statues are too numerous to count, though I can recall a few which have made a special impression upon me: a king, sitting slumped in his throne; a mermaid perched on a rock; a maiden with seashells in her hair. These statues are all rendered in such immaculate detail that they seem to be more living things, magicked to stillness, than objects carved from stone.

I walk through the halls and observe still more statues. There are great glass windows, through which I can see the shifting green waters of the sea. It is a sunken palace, a forgotten structure between the waves. With each dream I strive further, exploring more of this mysterious palace. I have found thus far a library of waterlogged books, and a greenhouse where a number of the most exquisite white flowers grow.

I must confess that I am stunned that my own imagination could conjure such a vast and elaborate fantasy! I am eager now for each night of sleep, anticipating the chance to see more of the world my mind has built for itself. My favorite of all the statues is that of a knight robed in armor, kneeling penitently and holding a single rose. I feel emanating from him a sense of nobility, of sacrifice, and of love. He is a hero who will rescue the girl in the tower and swear to her his unyielding devotion. He will cut away the thorns that ensnare her; he will wake her from her infinite slumber with a kiss.

I have begun to take great solace in these dreams, Clementina. Where I have not known such love in the waking world, I can indulge in it now; I can drown myself in it. This is not the life I planned for myself when we were girls, giggling and braiding daisy chains—I had never imagined I would be twenty-eight and a spinster, with little else to show for my time on earth than some contributions to my father's work that will never be acknowledged.

And yet . . . I can still dream. This is a power that no man, no mortal force, can take from me. While the sickness corrodes my body, it has left my mind untouched.

So here I am, in some ways still the girl I was all those years ago, hoping, believing. I am feeling quite well just now. When I close my eyes, I see that grand palace, those statues with their mysterious virtues, their pulsating sentiments; indeed, their love. Their beauty is all around me.

I must mark this as a peaceful and happy hour.

Affectionately yours,
A.A.

Uncovering Angharad: An Inquiry into the Authorship of Major Works Attributed to Emrys Myrddin

by EUPHEMIA SAYRE and PRESTON HÉLOURY

ABSTRACT: Emrys Myrddin, known best for his seminal work *Angharad* as well as various poems, is, by the metric of book sales, the most commercially successful author in Llyr's history. He is also acclaimed by critics and widely studied in academic circles, all factors that have led to his recent inauguration as Llyr's seventh Sleeper. This paper argues that, following the discovery of decades-old correspondence and diary entries, his authorship of these works must be seriously questioned. These materials, which have been independently vetted by numerous scholars and investigated by the editorial board of Llyr's newspaper of record, prove that the bulk of Myrddin's work was written by his wife, Angharad Myrddin, née Blackmar, and that a long and abiding conspiracy involving both Myrddin and other members of his literary circle has attempted to suppress this. This paper proves that *Angharad*, and its illustrious legacy, must be correctly attributed to Mrs. Myrddin, for the sake of scholarship's commitment to absolute truth and the University of Llyr's adherence to its motto, "Swear fealty to no cause but knowledge."

I Introduction

Most scholarship on *Angharad* and Myrddin's other works has both focused on and elided Myrddin's biography. Famously reclusive, the man's few interviews and scant biographical details

dangler

have provided much fodder for speculation and even imagination. "No other author in Llyr's history has evoked the academic's imagination quite like Myrddin," writes Dr. Cedric Gosse, widely considered the foremost expert on Myrddin's work and life. "Many of these supposed academic papers might be more properly considered fiction" (Gosse 199).

Much of this may be owed to the proclivity of Northern academics to view the South as a "fanciful realm of whimsy, trapped in a time long past, existing merely for Northern writers to project their fantasies upon" (Brinley 206). Indeed, while Myrddin himself was adamant that he did not wish to be considered a "Southern writer," his colleague and friend, Colin Blackmar, was quite happy to mine the "aesthetic and folkloric traditions of the South" (Brinley 206). Side by side, the works of Myrddin and Blackmar offer a fascinating, if divergent, framework for understanding Southern literature. Even more so when the lives of both authors—most certainly divergent—are considered, the first being of poor, rural Southern extraction, and the latter of wealthy Northern blood.

Yet with the political and academic hay that has been made of Myrddin's mysterious life, it is all the more baffling that his wife has never entered these scholarly conversations. Browsing the archives of journals and periodicals concerning Myrddin, we were not able to find a single work that mentioned his wife in more than a passing reference—and she was never once referred to by name. One is moved to consider, then, whether this elision is unconscious or part of active efforts to erase from conversation her potential influence over his corpus and his life. This is even more bizarre given that his wife shares her name with both the novel and protagonist of his most famous work: Angharad.

RIWAN
HÉLOURY
SO RUNS THIS TALE,
LIKE A STREAM
INTO THE SEA,
NOT TO FADE,
BUT TO CHANGE
AND BE FREE

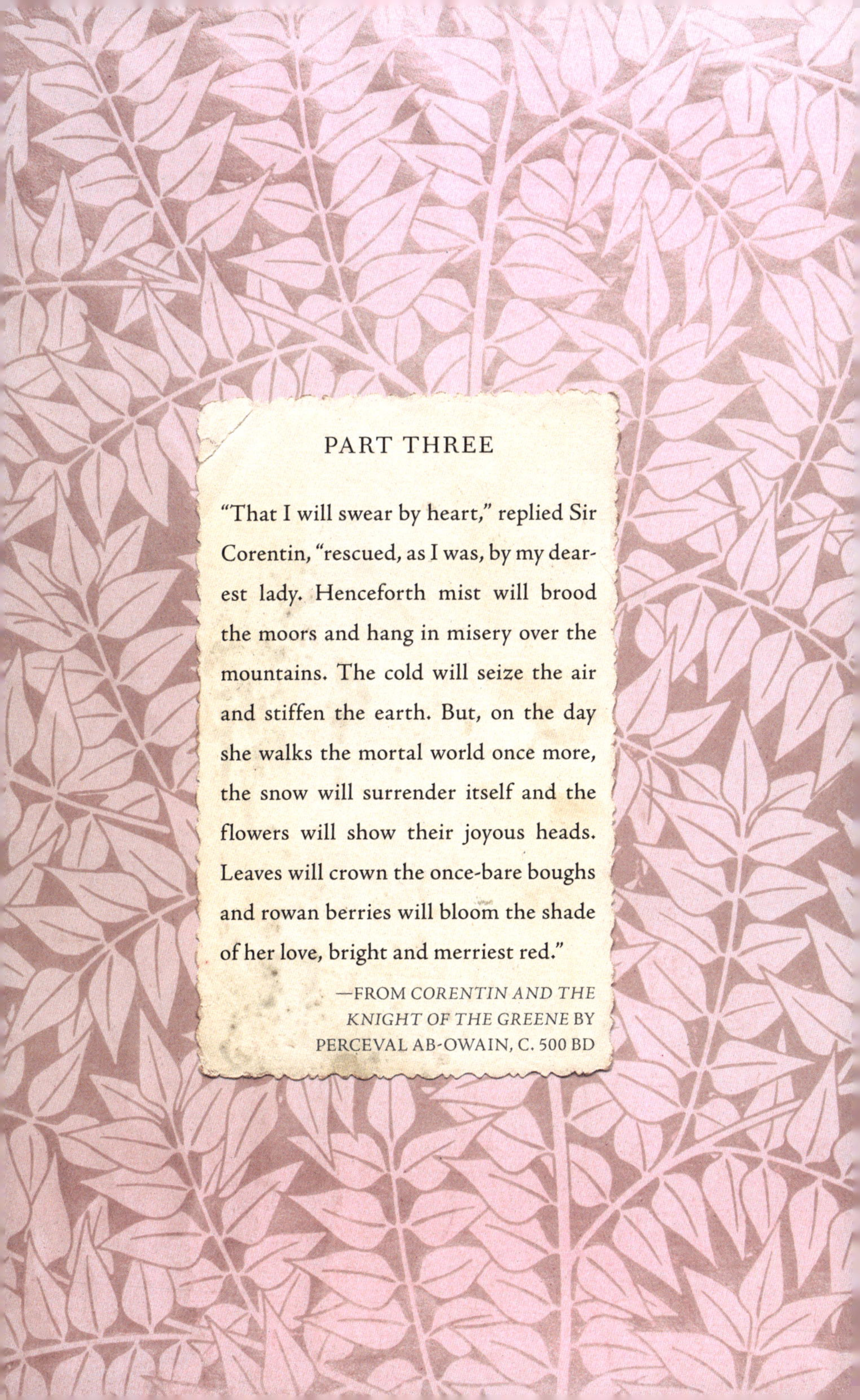

PART THREE

"That I will swear by heart," replied Sir Corentin, "rescued, as I was, by my dearest lady. Henceforth mist will brood the moors and hang in misery over the mountains. The cold will seize the air and stiffen the earth. But, on the day she walks the mortal world once more, the snow will surrender itself and the flowers will show their joyous heads. Leaves will crown the once-bare boughs and rowan berries will bloom the shade of her love, bright and merriest red."

—FROM *CORENTIN AND THE KNIGHT OF THE GREENE* BY PERCEVAL AB-OWAIN, C. 500 BD

ONE

The snow began to fall and Effy felt a twinge of hope.

She had cloistered herself in the library for the morning—and the past *two* mornings—determined to make progress on her paper. She'd sat at the window in the pale glimmer of gray winter light, shoulder pressed against the cold glass, and written . . .

Nothing. Well, nothing of value, at least. She had some scribbled notes, half-legible, accompanied by far more impressive (and rather baroque) marginalia, of rowan berries and bridal dresses and gleaming silver gauntlets, darting ermines in their white camouflage. Of course, she could hardly turn those in to her literature professor, though they did represent the important motifs of her chosen subject matter: *Corentin and the Knight of the Greene.*

The paper was for her second-year seminar, which focused on the works of Perceval ab-Owain, the second Sleeper. *Corentin,* like much of the rest of his corpus, concerned some of the earliest legends of Llyr, replete with fairies and brave mortal women and passionate, kneeling knights.

All of Effy's favorite things. Which was why she was so frustrated by her lack of progress. Surely, *surely*, she could find a profound paper topic, an impressive thesis statement, bold and novel and groundbreaking. And yet, for days, it had eluded her.

But now, with the snow gathering, soft and sugar-white on the windowsill, she thought that perhaps it would inspire her. After all, *Corentin* was a decidedly wintry tale, celebrating the cycle of death and rebirth, the dawning of the new year. Well, she could start there, at least . . . with a summary of the work and its author.

"Corentin and the Knight of the Greene" is considered to be the consummate work of Perceval ab-Owain, Llyr's second Sleeper and the author of many other acclaimed chivalric romances. Corentin concerns the titular character, a knight, and his love, Florimell. While they are preparing for their wedding, on the eve of the new year, Florimell is ensorcelled and abducted by the Knight of the Greene, a sinister and beguiling fairy. He tells Corentin that he must find him in the Greene—the realm of the fae—and rescue his bride. However, in a surprising subversion of the genre's typical tropes, Florimell is able to escape her captor, saving Corentin in the process . . .

TWO

There was something, at least. Effy tapped her pen impatiently against her notebook—and then saw the time on her wristwatch.

She had an appointment in ten minutes, and she could not afford to be late. She hurriedly crammed her journal and her copy of *Corentin* back into her satchel and rushed out of the library, out into the crisply cold morning and the gently lilting snow.

A DREAMY DAY IN ARGANT

Modern weddings in Argant are a whimsical blend of folklore, traditional religion, and more practical customs. The bridal stole, for example, typically made of ermine fur, was a historical necessity, worn to protect against the bitter mountain cold. These mantles have now become elaborate, featuring fringes and lace detailing, and are often worn in the place of veils. As is traditional, the stole is given one final symbolic stitch on the eve of the wedding, to represent the addition of a new bride into the family.

The most straightforwardly religious aspect of the ceremony is the stone-casting: on the altar there is a silver chalice, filled with water, and the bride and the groom must each place one white stone and one black

within it. The black represents Ankou, the shade, and the white Lutine, the saint. Lutine will bless the couple with a long life, and Ankou will grant them a peaceful death, guiding them to eternal rest hand in hand.

The last and most fantastical element of the ceremony concerns the legends of the fairies ("fées"), which, in Argant, are said to dwell exclusively in the sea caves and grottoes. They take the form of beautiful women with long golden hair, and, unlike the fairies of the folkloric traditions of our neighbors to the south, they are not malicious. Indeed, they often gift mortals with magic items: a spool of thread that never runs out, enchanted ships that cannot sink. It is said that their voices are so sweet and melodious that merely hearing a few notes of their song is enough to cause a man to fall in love.

"Comme une fée, pour ta beauté."

"Like a fairy for your beauty."

So, as is tradition, the groom closes his eyes as the bride approaches the altar. He does not open them until he hears her voice. Then, when he looks upon her at last, he says, "Comme une fée pour ta beauté." ("Like a fairy for your beauty.") ❦

THREE

It was the first *true* snow of winter, more than the dusting that had briefly covered the lintels of the library and the statue outside the literature college in a pale, brittle cloak. These flakes were lush and heavy, and Effy paused for a moment to look up. The sky was a charcoal sketch, white against gray, like the kind she might idly draw in her notepad.

She wouldn't be able to capture the briskness of the air, though, or the intangible, almost electric force that made all her fellow students tip their heads back to watch the snow fall, childlike again in their wonder. The *magic*. Things always felt more fanciful this time of year.

But Effy couldn't linger in its spell. She was already—*mortifyingly*—late.

The shop was all silk and lace, and a welcome relief from the cold. She felt less than relieved, however, when she saw Rhia standing by the door, arms crossed over her chest and an exasperated look on her face.

"It's twelve past two," she said.

"Don't tell me *you've* become an enforcer of punctuality." Effy tried to sound nobly defiant. "You're as bad as Preston now."

"Only when it concerns fashion."

"A virtuous cause, to be sure."

"Oh, come on," Rhia said, tugging Effy by the elbow. "I've already picked out a few."

Of course she had. She allowed Rhia to maneuver her through the aisles, past bloated gowns of tulle that looked rather like snowdrifts that had blown into the shop. Satin massed upon satin, chiffon upon crepe. As they walked, Rhia kept up a steady stream of chatter, schooling Effy on the subtle differences between ivory and eggshell, which was apparently essential knowledge.

By the time they reached the shop's back room, Effy was beginning to think she might prefer line scansion.

"Here," Rhia said, trilling the *r* and dramatically sweeping out her arm. "I've selected a dozen preliminary options. Once you decide on skirt length, neckline, fabric, and silhouette, we can start narrowing them down."

Effy reached toward the nearest gown, fingering the long lace sleeves. "These seem practical," she said. "It's going to be freezing."

"Who cares about practical? This is your *wedding*."

Effy bit back a smile. "Well, I suppose I'll allow myself a bit of extravagance. And really, I shouldn't have to worry about the cold. There's a tradition, in Argant, to wear a white-furred mantle over your gown. Preston's mother is bringing hers for me. It's a family heirloom."

"That sounds lovely."

"I hope I deserve it." Effy glanced down at her hands; she rarely thought about her missing finger anymore, except in those moments when she also remembered what it was intended for. Instinctually, she reached for the silver chain around her throat. The ring was there, safe, bundled beneath her scarf.

"Don't be silly," Rhia said. "No one has to earn the right to be loved. And if you ask me, *he's* the lucky one."

Softly, Effy laughed. "Don't say that in your wedding toast, please."

"I won't. I'll just think it."

Then they set about sorting through the gowns, Rhia lacing her into one dress after another, laughing as they went. Rhia, with the resolute precision of a war general, kept a list of each one's merits and defects. And, eventually, Effy began to familiarize herself with terms like *tea-length* and *A-line* and *high-collar.*

As Effy regarded her reflection in the mirror, the skirt drifting around her and the pearl buttons gleaming at her throat, there was a sudden jolt in her stomach.

"I never thought I would get here," she said—quietly, almost a whisper. "I never . . . I never thought I would survive this long."

For all her dreaming, for all her years of wishing and hoping and believing in magic, she had never allowed herself to imagine this: the simple, quotidian joys of being human.

Rhia stepped over to her. Without speaking, she put her arms over Effy's shoulders and squeezed. Their faces in the mirror pressed together, Effy's gold hair mingling with Rhia's dark curls.

The silent embrace was more comforting than any words could have been. The two girls who looked back were just that: girls. No shadows in the corners of the room, no glaze of the unreal that blurred Effy's vision.

In some ways it had been easier to yearn for the impossible. But maybe now she was safe enough—brave enough—to want the ordinary.

FOUR

"Look," Lotto said. "It's snowing."

Preston glanced through the window. Indeed, flakes were drifting down gently from the sky, brushing against the glass like pale-winged moths. He stared for a moment, enraptured, moved by the inexplicable magic of the winter's first snow. But it was only for a moment: Lotto spoke again, and the spell released him.

"You know what this means," his friend was saying.

"Your deadline is rapidly approaching?"

Lotto groaned. "Have you no sense of childlike wonder?"

"I'm getting married in a week," Preston replied. "I should hope I've put everything childish behind me."

"Well," Lotto said, rather sullen now, "I was going to say that it means tomorrow will be the annual snowball fight, but now that you've reminded me—*you're* on a deadline, too, professor. Have you written your vows yet?"

"I'm not a professor."

"You have a class now, and students." Lotto took a dramatic swig of his tea, draining the cup to its dregs.

"It's just an introductory language class," said Preston. "And I'm an instructor, not a professor."

"Close enough."

"You need a doctorate to be a professor. That's years and years away."

He'd only just begun his doctoral program, after graduating in the summer. His and Effy's thesis had been published by the *Llyrian Times*, and then in a number of academic journals, to equal parts praise and repudiation. There had been the irate letter from Greenebough Publishing, idly threatening legal action. ("An empty threat," the *Times*'s editorial director had assured him. "We've been sued by bigger buffoons before.") There had been the reporters, tailing them throughout campus, until Dean Fogg issued a statement that any non-student or non–faculty member who set foot on the campus would be risking arrest.

It would have all been worth it anyway, to have Angharad's story told. But, in the end, they had won: sculptors were in the process of chiseling Myrddin's name off the lintel of the literature college.

Preston's grades and the momentous reception of the thesis would have been enough to admit him to the doctoral program—but there was one last unexpected gift.

Their meeting on the pier had been the last time Preston saw Master Gosse. The next day, he tendered his resignation to Dean Fogg. Within the hour, his office was cleared out entirely. All that was left behind was a single envelope with Preston's name written on it.

Inside was a letter of recommendation, addressed to the admissions office of the literature college. Only one line.

You could hardly DREAM of a more able student.

Within the empty office, Preston had laughed to himself.

Now, Lotto's voice broke him from his reverie once more.

". . . if you wanted, we could swap, you know. In the academic field your talents have always surpassed mine. But when it comes to romance . . ."

Preston realized that he was talking about the vows. He gave Lotto a sardonic smile. "Thank you for the offer. But I think the whole point of wedding vows is to be sincere and earnest."

"Am I not sincere and earnest?"

"You've lied to Professor Damlet six times to get an extension."

"Oh," Lotto conceded. He looked down at his empty cup. "Right. That."

Even with Preston's help and with his father's many generous financial contributions, there was no hope of Lotto completing his university degree in the requisite three years. So Lotto was in his fourth year, making slow progress toward his degree, but still as roguish as ever.

Truthfully, Preston was glad that nothing had broken Lotto's puckish spirit. He took a sip of his own coffee and said, "Do you want help? I can start an outline—"

"No, it's all right," Lotto said. "You have plenty else on your mind."

Fair enough, Preston thought. With a scant seven days until the wedding, he still had not written his vows, despite half a dozen false starts. He realized as he glanced down that he had been scribbling ideas on his napkin, opening lines that were either far too maudlin or far too contrived and highbrow. Nothing that captured the way he truly felt when he looked at Effy. He was frustrated by his persistent failures. What was the point in all his studying, all his showy academic accomplishments, if he couldn't articulate what was most important?

He crumpled up the napkin.

Since the very first moment I—
There is a quote from—
I am the furthest thing from a poet, but—

FIVE

The dress fit perfectly. A sign, Effy thought. She carried it, carefully wrapped in plastic and then folded inside a shopping bag, through the streets of Caer-Isel, her breath pluming white in the cold. She walked through the literature college courtyard, past the students who smoked persistently under the eaves, no matter the caprices of the weather, snow gathering like powdered sugar on their dark wool coats.

She recognized one of them from her seminar; he paused between drags and waved.

Effy waved back, and for a moment was struck by the surreal quality of the interaction. A year ago, any sort of acknowledgment from one of her fellow students would have terrified her. Her mind would have thrown up a thousand questions (*What did he see? Does he know? Is he mocking me?*) that all would have pricked her like needles, until she ran away and numbed the fear with pills.

Now . . . the fears were not quite gone—perhaps they never

would be—but they were contained. A faint bristle against her skin, the brief uptick of her pulse, and then no more. She let them pass, like a whisper on the wind.

Effy had far more urgent concerns anyway. She hurried to her flat, unlocked the door, and stamped the snow from her boots. She hung the dress in her closet—still in its plastic sheath, so Preston would not catch a look—and then slumped down at the table.

After a moment, and with a labored sigh, she removed the books from her satchel. Her sketchpad, her journal, and her dog-eared, marked-up copy of *Corentin*. Her wedding was in seven days, but it was another romance that vexed her.

As she sulked, a white petal drifted down and settled on the cover. Preston had gotten into the habit of buying her winter camellias, a new bouquet every week. Effy often came home to see another vase on the table, with fresh and sweet-smelling flowers.

She wasn't sure what had begotten this tradition. Of all flowers, why winter camellias? What did they symbolize? There was a vague sense of recognition, a flicker, as if once Effy *had* known, but the full truth eluded her. A memory, lost to time.

It didn't much matter. She plucked up the petal and it slipped between her fingers, velvet-soft.

The door opened, bringing in a waft of cold. Effy turned to see Preston, hair damp, glasses askew, and face flushed. The collar and the whole front of his coat was crusted in snow.

"Oh," Effy said, trying to manage her shock. "What happened?"

"Lotto," he replied.

"Naturally."

"He insisted that a snowball fight is a requisite part of enjoying winter."

"Oh," Effy said again. She blinked. "It doesn't look like it was much of a fight."

"It was more like an ambush." Preston shook off his coat. "Years of rugby have whetted his battle instincts, I suppose."

Effy rose to help him. "And he didn't consider how unbecoming it would be for a groom to show up to his wedding with a broken nose?"

"No. He was merciless." Preston smiled. He let Effy slip him out of his coat and hang it on the rack. He brushed his damp hair from his forehead before saying, "Speaking of incorrigible acquaintances . . . did Rhia help you find a dress?"

"Yes," Effy replied, and brightened a bit. "She was very disgruntled that I'd waited until the very last moment, but she was a big help. We found one that fits perfectly. No alterations. Like it was meant to be. My procrastination goes unpunished once again."

"Perfect." Preston kissed her gently on the bridge of her nose, his lips still faintly chill from the cold.

"If only I'd been so lucky with my other project of the day."

Pulling away, Preston frowned. "What is that?"

Effy sighed again, heavily. She went over to the table and plucked up her copy of *Corentin*, the leather cover loose at its binding and threatening to break free. The tattered state of it, at least, reflected how she felt.

"My paper is due the day after the wedding," she explained.

"But I haven't even figured out a thesis statement yet. I spent the whole morning at the library, and still . . . nothing. Well, nothing except for some crude marginalia."

"Do you mind if I take a look?"

Effy handed him the worse-for-wear tome. Preston flipped through the pages, the little furrow between his brow appearing as he stared down in concentration. Effy loved the way he looked in these moments: utterly serious, fixed to his task, a true scholar at heart.

He'd read it before, of course—surely there were very few books remaining in the world that *hadn't* read—but that did not mean he approached the task with any less seriousness. He pushed his glasses up the bridge of his nose, another familiar gesture that filled her heart with warmth and affection.

"It's been a long time," he admitted when he looked up from the book at last, "but it's more moving than I recall. One of the more, well, *romantic* Romances."

"You've gone so soft, Preston Héloury."

The corner of his mouth quirked up. "Maybe so. I don't suppose you'd consider a stylistic angle. Meter and rhyme. A—forgive me—formalist approach."

Effy wrinkled her nose.

"I thought not." Preston flipped another page. "What about intertextuality? There are a lot of works directly inspired by *Corentin*. 'The Garden in Stone,' for one."

"I think I've had enough of Ardor," Effy replied. "And, it seems, well . . . too easy. Just comparing one work to another. Hasn't it been done a thousand times before?"

Preston's gaze was soft with fondness. "You don't have to set the literary world on fire with every paper, Effy. Don't be so hard on yourself."

"You have to admit," Effy said, "that my first paper has set the bar rather high."

"Fair enough." Preston let out an amused breath. "But something will come to you. It always does."

"I hope so." She took *Corentin* from him and set it back down on the table, beside the shedding winter camellias. "Is everything else in order now? The venue, the decorations . . ."

"Yes," Preston replied—but there was something strange in his tone, a catch of breath? "My mother and brother will arrive on Friday. And the church has been booked for the ceremony, and the restaurant for the reception."

Effy nodded, though a familiar sensation of guilt wriggled through her stomach. "Are you sure it's all right that I didn't invite them?"

Preston knew who she meant—they'd had this conversation no less than a dozen times in the past several weeks.

"Of course it's all right," he said. "It's *your* wedding. No one should be there unless you want them there. Just because they're family doesn't mean you owe them anything."

"I know."

It was easy to say—harder to believe. She had not invited her mother to her wedding, nor her grandparents, and there were no other relatives to speak of. It was not for lack of trying, though.

Month after excruciating month Effy had willed herself to pick up the phone, to mail the invitation, but something had always stopped her. Every time, she remembered her mother's voice on the other line, that bitter, wintry night a year ago.

Just because you love her doesn't mean you can save her.

She was no longer that child alone on the riverbank, but her mother had never stopped abandoning her, in one little way after another.

And her grandparents . . . no matter how much time Effy had spent with them, they still felt as unreachable as distant stars. Her grandfather locked in his office, behind that gleaming wooden desk that always seemed enormously tall, her grandmother in the kitchen, her gaze passing over Effy in silent exasperation, as if she were no more than a cat or a houseplant. They had not cared for her; they had administered to her. She had their attention, but never their love.

She could not think of it without feeling a lump form in her throat. But then, as had become her instinct, she reached for the chain that held her wedding ring and squeezed it. It was a reminder she carried with her that she *was* wanted.

That she was loved.

Effy pushed herself up onto her tiptoes and kissed Preston on the mouth. He slid his arms around her waist and pulled her against him. And then *Corentin,* and the flowers, and the dress, and the snow, and even, for a moment, the wedding itself, was forgotten.

CORENTIN
AND THE KNIGHT OF THE GREENE
Perceval ab-Owain

SIX

The week wore on, colder and snowier by the hour. The streets were slick with ice, making the cobblestones glimmer where the lamplight shone, in pools of limpid gold. Each morning at the library Effy faced down her paper like a warrior, girded and braced, only instead of sword and shield she wielded pen and paper.

And yet she might have been more successful with a blade. Her pen still produced little more than idle scribbling and marginalia. She had taken to copying her favorite passages from *Corentin* into her notebook, hoping that it might kindle some spark of inspiration.

Fairest of face she was, with hair like spun gold, yet it was her manner, more so than her form, that beguiled the knight. So light were her steps upon the earth, as though she feared to disturb any living creature, or even the soil itself; willow trees bent their branches toward her as she walked, and rabbits peered with large dark eyes from their burrows, and the song of the birds seemed to become a wordless hymn, an ode to the loveliest and gentlest Lady Florimell.

The beauty of the words impressed themselves on Effy, and she felt a deep sense of gratitude that at last she was able to study them. That her mind, and her heart, could be moved with passion toward her chosen field. So many years she had longed for this, and now she was here.

And she was not the only one. That morning, Effy had to cut her morose and seemingly fruitless musing short. She left the library, *Corentin* tucked, as ever, in her satchel, and made her way to the Drowsy Poet.

When she entered, taking a brief moment to bask in the cafe's pleasant warmth, Effy cast her gaze over the room, searching. Among the students with their shoulders bowed over books and the workers from nearby shops enjoying their afternoon breaks, Effy spotted a familiar head of dark, glossy hair.

Effy maneuvered her way around the tables and dropped down into the seat across from her. Maeve looked up from beneath her bangs and smiled.

"Hi," she said, a faint flush rising to her cheeks. "Sorry, um, I should have ordered you something."

"Don't worry about it," Effy said. "I didn't mean to keep you waiting. I was working on a paper and lost track of time at the library."

"Oh," said Maeve. She seemed to brighten slightly, her shy smile deepening. "What's the paper on?"

Effy had to smile back, charmed by her earnestness. Maeve Guilford was a first-year literature student, and the inaugural recipient of Angharad's scholarship. She had written her application essay on the depiction of Queen Tria in Tristram Marlais's play *Tria: A Tragedie*. Her writing had startled Effy by being so stylish and so self-assured, and by contrasting, quite poignantly, Tria's narrative arc with the portrayals of female characters in the works of Marlais's contemporaries. Among hundreds of applicants, Maeve had clearly distinguished herself.

In person, Maeve was rather more diffident and restrained, though perhaps that had more to do with her circumstances than her natural temperament. She was only the second-ever woman admitted to the literature college, still a precarious position even after Dean Fogg's official decree. The awareness of it seized Effy at moments, too, making her stomach clutch with anxiety and her nerve endings spark like live wires.

But Effy was determined that Maeve would not have the same experiences she'd had. She would not allow her to be maligned, to be shamed, to be cowed. For the first several weeks she had walked Maeve to and from all of her classes, had accompanied her to the bookstore to purchase her required texts, and had even shown her the coziest, remotest alcoves in the library, where she could study undisturbed. She and Maeve and Rhia had eaten together at the dining hall each night, with Maisie relenting to join them once or twice.

By midwinter, Maeve had begun to shed some of her shyness, and Effy's own anxiety abated, too. Now, when they met once a week for coffee, it was a purely social occasion—not a precautionary assignation. Maeve's presence was fading into the safety of mundanity. Another wonderful, utterly ordinary part of her life that Effy could hardly have conceived of even a year ago.

Effy's own smile deepened, thinking about it. About how, in some respects, all was well. Then she shook her head, as if to clear it, and replied, "It's on *Corentin and the Knight of the Greene*. Have you read it?"

Maeve nodded. "There was an abridged version in one of my primary schoolbooks—you know, with all the prose made simple and accessible for nine-year-olds. But the church nearest to my house was dedicated to Saint Florimell. So I read the real, full version at Sunday school."

"I don't suppose you have any ideas for a paper topic."

"No. Sorry." Maeve laughed softly. "I think my most enduring impression was that I wanted to dress up as Florimell for the summer solstice festival. You know, a crown of rowan berries in my hair . . ."

"That's the perfect solstice costume," Effy said.

"It *would* have been, but my brother refused to dress up as Corentin. We're twins, so our parents always made us wear matching costumes. We ended up going as Calidore and Cambina. War and peace. So trite."

Effy let memories of the summer solstice rise in the theater behind her eyelids. The flower garlands draped on every portico and storefront awning, the white maypole rising against the clear azure sky. "I always dressed up as Angharad."

Maeve peered at her from behind her thick-framed glasses. "I can definitely see the resemblance."

To the woman, or to the character? Effy didn't ask. They were one and the same. She had carried book-Angharad in her head for so long, and now it was the real Angharad who walked beside her. There was strength in both. The power of reality and of imagination.

Something flickered to life in Effy's mind. The beginnings of an idea, inarticulable at the moment. Instead of reaching for paper and pen, she let the thoughts flow, washing over her as gently as the low tide. Dreams and materiality. Truth and fantasy. Their marriage—literal and figurative, laced together like a handfasting.

A part of her wanted to bolt up from the table and return to the library, to desperately and hurriedly scratch out these novel epiphanies. But Preston's voice echoed in her mind. *You don't have to set the literary world on fire with every paper.*

No, she conceded, she did not. Funny to think, after all this time, that she had to impress this upon herself: there was more to life than literature and scholarship. Wisdom and reason could only matter so much when the alternative was love.

Effy settled back into her seat, allowing her heart to fill with fondness and her mouth to fill with laughter.

TRIA: Garb me in my laurels and array me in my cloth of gold,

I am queen of the winter, when the earth lies down in darkness and cold;

I am mistress of the spring blooms, hyacinth and daffodil;

I am consort of Quirinus, the god who rouses the summer wheat from fallow fields;

I am empress of the autumn, my temper like the ever-changing leaves.

If nature can bow to a woman's command, then why not man?

Must I shrink from your passions and rages like a cringing sheep?

Can I not be, myself, spitfire and fishwife, harpy and fire-eater,

She-wolf and hell-cat?

I shall relent to no man's temper, no brutish weapon or animal strength.

No raving or fretting, or stamping of feet.

I shall lie down before the hearth of one virtue: love.

If you wish to tame me, as you would some fantastical beast,

Unicorn or lioness,

Then you will first place your own heart on a platter,

And allow me to consume.

LEANDER: Great lady, great queen,

I would lie down in winter and rise,

As a dead man from the underworld,

When your beauty makes the flowers bloom.

SEVEN

Everything had been arranged. The venue and the flowers, the food and the photographer, the stiff black suit that hung in the back of his closet, and the mysterious, paper-wrapped gown of Effy's that hung beside it. His mother and brother would arrive that evening. All preparations had been undertaken, all potential crises accounted for. He should have felt nothing but uninhibited joy. And yet . . .

His vows still eluded him. For days Preston had hardly slept, instead watching Effy as she slumbered beside him, her bare arms gleaming white in the moonlight, her golden hair given a cast of silver. It would be easy to praise her beauty, the way it knocked the breath from him, as if every time he saw her was the first time. Eyes like green fire. Half real and half a fairy tale.

That morning he had arisen early, while Effy still slept, and left a note for her explaining that he'd gone to the library to prepare for that day's class. His students were reading *Dunstan's*

Hymn in the original Old Llyrian, and Preston did need to brush up. But on his way to the library, he found himself wandering instead toward the pier.

It was a still and quiet morning, all the snow on the streets and rooftops frozen into shining sheets of ice. Even in the deepest heart of winter, the temperatures in Llyr did not approach the lowest temperatures of Argant, so Preston was well insulated against the cold. Dawn glimmered at the line of the horizon, soft yellows and pale pinks against the lingering darkness of night.

He strode to the pier's very end and leaned over the railing, bracing himself on his elbows. The frozen surface of Lake Bala had cracked, black veins showing themselves between the ice floes. The mountains of Argant rose up clear and sharp in the distance, unobstructed by the clouds. By now his mother and brother had already left, boarding a train to Caer-Isel. He would meet them at the station in the afternoon.

Preston cast his gaze slightly to the west.

What had once been was no more. All the remains of the Sleeper Museum had been cleared away; some of it that could not easily be moved had been burned, the ashes scattered into the water. Most of the colossal wreckage was beneath the waves, irretrievable, the corpses now slumbering (dreaming?) in their seafloor tomb. There was currently a hearty debate among members of parliament about what should be done with the property. Conservatives and warhawks argued that it should be made into a museum that showcased Argant's crimes and the belligerent history between the two nations. Liberals proposed that it should be turned into a memorial for the dead.

Preston recalled a quote from one of the letters of Tristram Marlais. *They are afraid to accept that a king can die. They are afraid to accept that, in the end, all kings must.* He had woken up, and he was confident that the rest of Llyr would soon follow. No more dreams, and no more nightmares.

More memories flooded him. He had stood in precisely this place with Effy, when they had first returned from Hiraeth. When he had first told her about the bells. She had looked at him so quizzically, bemused and in shock. He was still yet to believe in magic. But Effy was, as always, a step ahead of him.

It had felt like the end, then—the mystery of Myrddin solved, Angharad freed, he and Effy both safe, and in love. Now he knew it had only been the start. There was still so much left to do.

He had proposed to her in this exact place, too. Kissed her as the seabirds dipped and whirled, as the waves turned green and gold in the sunlight. The memories seemed to layer over each other; he saw them both at once, as if outside his own body and looking down. Effy's hair, unfurling in the wind, just as it had when they'd walked along the cliffs in Saltney. When he had felt his chest ache with longing and his stomach clench with the fear that he'd never get to hold her, to touch her.

The corners of his eyes began to burn. Preston touched them, and his thumb came away damp.

It came to him so suddenly, then, like the crashing of the tide against the shore. The words had been there all along. He had only needed to remember.

Alight with inspiration, Preston turned hurriedly and walked down the pier. The ice groaned and cracked, and the waves sang at his back. He half ran to his flat, sky brightening in increments overhead, hoping that by the time he arrived Effy would still be asleep. *Dunstan's Hymn* would have to wait.

The Knight of the Greene caressed the cheek of his dear Florimell; his bony fingers trailed through her long golden hair. Pale was her face, full of fear, and her dress shuddered about her as if it were possessed of its own spirit. The Knight was a fairy of great power, matched only by his covetousness; such was the nature of his kind. For a creature that could never change, could never grow, the fragile and moribund essence of humanity was of so much wonderment to him. Her brief and flickering life was made all the more beautiful because it was doomed.

Florimell touched a hand to her mouth. To her lover, Corentin, who stood at a distance, she said, "I will return, when the year turns over, when the snow melts and the rowan berries are in bloom."

The Knight, with his sickly green countenance, with his beard of ivy and foliage, grasped Florimell by the arm, and both were gone. All that remained with Corentin was love, which was as agonizing as it was tenacious, as wistful as it was steadfast. He had in mind to rescue his lady, but he could not see how; his heart was lost to ardor, and to grief. If he could not fight, could not follow the Knight to his Greene, then he would wait in this place, till he turned to stone, till lichen grew over him and his armor scabbed with rust. His love would not be proven by action; it would be proven by patience. This virtue oft overlooked, yet so essential.

EIGHT

The library again. Only now, her muscles were not taut with anxiety, her teeth no longer grinding in frustration. At the very last moment, the idea had come, miraculous in its wholeness and eloquence. With *Corentin* by her side, her notebook open on her lap, Effy began to write.

The prevailing scholarship on "Corentin" focuses on its themes of nature, death, and rebirth. When composed, in approximately 500 BD, Llyr was a largely rural, agricultural nation, and the turning of the seasons was significant to Llyrian way of life. The new year marked the end of the fallow period and the nearing of the harvest. The romantic sheen that ab-Owain applies to this tale is largely considered to illustrate the importance of these cycles of death and rebirth.

The return of Florimell—modern-day saint of agriculture—is met with both joy and relief. That Corentin waits for her, rather than attempting her rescue, symbolizes the stiffening grasp of winter, a period of stillness where animals hibernate in their dens and humans hunker down in their homes and weather the cold. But there is more to this narrative choice. "Corentin" is, in some respects, an early example of a "fairy ballad," the preeminent form of literary romance.

Reading "Corentin" as a proto-ballad unlocks a new angle to the story and opens up pathways for novel analysis. One of the most notable and relatively unique elements of "Corentin" is that Florimell rescues herself, returning to the material world as promised, and bringing with her the hopeful blossoming of spring. One can easily see the parallels between modern and contemporary romances—perhaps most significant among them being "Angharad".

Is it reductive to say that every story is a love story? Some scholars may think so. Yet every great work of Llyrian literature has its own glimmer of romance. From King Neirin and his liege-man to the errant-knight and the lady of Laurence Ardor's "Garden," from Tria and Leander to Florimell and Corentin, perhaps there is no greater unifying theme than that of love.

NINE

When Effy looked in the mirror, three faces looked back at her. Rhia, mouth held taut in concentration; Angharad, her silver hair in its glossy bob; and her own—cheeks patted with blush, lips daubed in a pale and dusty pink, which Rhia claimed was in her *color season*, and hair held back with what felt like a very precarious arrangement of pins. She had been perched at Rhia's vanity for so long that her legs were starting to ache.

"*Almost* finished," Rhia assured her.

Effy shifted her position, wincing, but not wanting to appear ungrateful. "I can't wait to see the masterpiece."

"Oh, I think this is my best work yet."

"Next time I need my hair done, I'm coming to Caer-Isel," Angharad said teasingly. "You've put my stylists to shame."

"If my music career doesn't take off, at least I have a backup plan." Rhia smiled. "Maisie would *love* that."

Effy laughed at the thought. "She's being inordinately patient now, though."

"Even she knows not to rush perfection," Rhia replied archly. With one last jab of a pin, she stepped back, leaving Effy alone in front of the mirror. "Done. Let me know what you think."

It took Effy a moment to steel herself before she looked. It was another experience that felt surreal in its ordinariness—dressing for her wedding. She knew, when she stared into the mirror, there would be no Fairy King at her back, no darkness in the corners of her vision. She would just see a girl, any girl, every girl.

And what a joy it was, to be like other girls.

When Effy dared to look at last, she was awestruck. If anything, Rhia had been too modest. Her eyelids were painted a shimmery white, surrounded by thick, fluttering dark lashes that had been so carefully glued to her lash line. Her brows were brushed into perfect shape. Yet there was a lightness to it all, a naturalness, her features augmented rather than disguised.

But her hair was indisputably the centerpiece. The front of it was pulled away from her face, then fluffed to a rather impressive height in the back. Curlers and hot tongs had sculpted it into loose waves. Among the whorls of gold, Rhia had pinned dozens of tiny satin bows, ivory and blush pink.

And flowers. Delicate, lacy sprigs of infant's breath; small, just-budding winter camellias. Effy had idly mentioned her love for them only once, but clearly Rhia had remembered. A tightness formed in her chest, affection clutching at her heart. She leaned over, wrapping her arms around Rhia's waist.

"Careful," Rhia chided her. "Don't smudge my masterpiece."

"You're a genius," Effy said. "It really is perfect. Thank you."

She rose from her seat on slightly wobbly legs. But it was not nervousness, not really. She was overcome with the knowledge that she could love and be loved in return. That even with her burdened head and fearful heart, she could feel such a glorious and mundane thing.

Angharad lifted the white fur stole from where it hung on the rack and, so very gently, pinned it over Effy's shoulders. It was fringed in lace and lined in the most exquisite seed pearls. Six generations of Argantian tradition, placed on Effy's back. Yet it didn't feel like a burden. It felt like a privilege.

She turned and regarded herself in the mirror one last time. The skirt of her gown flared out and ended just above her ankles, fluttery layers of broderie. It was belted at the waist and buttoned all the way to her throat. Effy watched herself smile, soft but uninhibited.

"I'm ready," she whispered. And then, again: "I'm ready."

TEN

The stained-glass windows of the Chapel of Saint Florimell were shimmery with fallen snow. The scene depicted was one of Florimell herself, rising from the underworld and bringing green spring with her, flowers blooming at her feet and birds landing light upon her shoulders. She wore a white gown, her golden hair unbound.

Preston had made concessions to the traditions of Llyr, just as Effy honored the traditions of Argant. He had no love for any saints—either Llyrian or Argantian—but Effy had pressed upon him the romantic nature of Florimell's myth. The unwilling fairy's bride, returning to her mortal lover.

And the church *was* beautiful. Preston had to concede that as well. The pews, gleaming dark wood, were draped in garlands of white flowers. The only light was what poured through the windows, illuminating the dais where he stood in a cast of palest gold.

It helped, too, that the pews were mostly empty. All the guests could easily be accommodated within the first two rows. Neither he nor Effy particularly relished being the center of attention, so the quietness and modesty of a small ceremony suited them. Only their most cherished friends and family were in attendance.

Preston let his gaze wander over the rows, lingering for a moment on each smiling face. His mother, her dark hair threaded with silver but her face still mostly unlined, stared up at him through wire-framed glasses that were identical to his own. Beside her, his brother, Ollie, tugged at his tie to loosen it. If Preston had their mother's face exactly, then Ollie had their father's.

Preston had known there would be a jolt of sadness, and he felt it now. The place where his father would have sat was empty. His chest tightened.

The grief was ruthless, but it was also a privilege. Though Preston didn't believe in god, didn't believe in the saints, didn't believe in ghosts, he still felt compelled to look up through the window to the obstructed sky, and let his mind supply the words that were very close to a prayer.

Da garout aran.

I love you.

It was Lotto's voice that startled him from his reverie, because of course it was. He sat beside Rhia and Maisie, and the three of them were fiercely whispering to each other. An argument, it seemed, but a good-natured one. When Lotto caught Preston looking, he dipped his head and gave a dazzlingly bright smile.

Before Preston could even smile back, the door to the church swept open.

Immediately, he closed his eyes. That was another Argantian

tradition that he relented to—mainly because of the folklore attached to it. In Argant, fairies were not sinister creatures; they were friends of mortals, often giving them magical boons, sometimes marrying them. They took the form of beautiful women and sang such beautiful songs that a mortal would fall in love upon hearing only their voices. Without ever seeing their beloved's face.

So Preston kept his eyes closed, listening to the patter of approaching footsteps. Two pairs—Effy's and Angharad's.

At last, the footsteps stopped, and Preston could sense Effy's nearness. The heat of her body, the soft, catching sound of her breath. Yet he waited a moment more, still on the dais, until he heard her say,

"I'm here."

He was as lovesick as any mortal man in the presence of his fairy bride. Her voice alone undid him. Preston opened his eyes at last, and, at once, his heart stammered in his chest.

It felt almost like a sin to call her beautiful—a disservice. She was a dream made manifest. If he had never believed in magic, never believed in fairy tales before, it was only because he hadn't met Effy yet.

She had walked down the aisle arm-in-arm with Angharad, and Preston dipped his head at the older woman in silent gratitude. She returned his nod and then released Effy, leaving to find her place in the pews.

When they were alone together at the altar, Preston's heart swelled. From under the mesh of her veil, Effy smiled at him. "So, have you fallen in love?"

"Since the first day I saw you," Preston replied. It sounded almost unbearably trite, but it was as honest as anything he'd ever said.

Effy shook her head good-naturedly. "No. You found me stubborn and insufferable."

"That doesn't mean I didn't love you." Preston bit his lip on a smile of his own. "And I can prove it to you."

An expression of bewilderment passed across her face as Preston reached toward the lectern behind them. He retrieved the package he had set upon it, until now hidden from Effy's sight.

Now, he held it out to her.

It was a book—sort of. Really, it was an album, with clear plastic folders instead of pages. As Effy opened it, a slight gasp rose from her lips.

Every page of the album was filled: with sketches, with diary entries, with letters, with photographs. There were even more mundane items: a ticket stub from his train ride to Saltney, a receipt from the pub where they'd first argued over Myrddin. There were snippets from *Angharad,* from Effy's favorite poems, which he'd carefully cut to fit. Some of them were cast-offs from her old books, with her careful annotations in the margins. Early drafts of their thesis, marked up with both of their commentaries.

Effy looked through it in silence for a moment. She paused for a moment at one page, where he'd slipped a piece of album artwork. "What is this?"

"It's from *Idylls & Canticles.*" Preston couldn't help but flush faintly. "'The Maiden of the North' is the song we danced to, at Penrhos. Do you remember?"

"Yes," she replied, her tone slightly strangled. "Of course."

Another page: a sketch Effy had done of the cliffs outside Hiraeth. She traced the drawing and then whispered, "I can't believe you saved these. All my silly little sketches . . . How did you even find them?"

"I hate to be the one to tell you this, but you're a bit of a packrat. You never throw anything away."

Effy laughed softly. "Well, I feel very justified in my hoarding tendencies now."

But the sketches were not what Preston really wanted her to see. As she paged further, a nervous knot rose in his throat. Absurd to be anxious about it now, with her standing before him in a bridal veil, but he felt it nonetheless. And when she came to the page—

"'Ridiculous,'" she read aloud. "'I despise every sentiment she has roused in me.'" Her brow furrowed in confusion. "What is this?"

"My journal entries," he replied, swallowing hard. "From Hiraeth."

Her gaze grew incredulous. She continued to read, her fingers trembling slightly as she turned each page. "'She's as infuriatingly stubborn as she is compellingly clever.'"

Preston felt himself flush again. "I was in denial. Clearly."

Another page turned. "'Effy Sayre is no vapid damsel. She is brilliant. And she might be the ruin of me yet.'" She looked up. "You really thought so?"

"Of course I did." His chest ached with fondness for her. "Keep reading."

Effy leafed through the album another few moments without speaking. When she looked up again, her green eyes were glossy. "'That's what she reminds me of: a fairy tale.'"

"You see?" Preston asked quietly. "I loved you from the beginning. And if you ever doubt it . . . just read through the book again. Everything you ever need to know is in here."

She ran her finger over the words *fairy tale*. "It all seems so simple, laid out like this."

"It is simple, Effy. It always has been."

Her eyes wavered, both clear and deep, like fire beneath the waves. Very gently, Preston folded the veil back, fully revealing her face. Even with their families and friends watching on from the pews, existence itself seemed to have narrowed to just the two of them, standing there on the altar. The white flowers strained toward the light that poured in from above. Snow fell softly against the stained-glass windows, and outside, the world was bright and new.

I was a very frightened person when I met you. I always have been—that isn't much of a secret. For a long time, I believed that was all I was: terror and survival. Quivering and fleeing. Cringing and hiding. I lived in fantasy because I couldn't bear reality. The painful and mundane cruelties of the world.

I never allowed myself to hope that something might draw me back—or give me a safe place to land. From the beginning, you were never afraid. You loved me like it was the easiest thing you'd ever done, as natural to you as breathing. And I came to think—I came to believe—that it really was.

You're patient. You're kind. You're brave, and more brilliant than I can put to words. The more time has passed, the more lucky I feel to be loved by you. My safety, my comfort, my protector, and now, my home. My family. You're someone I can hold on to when I feel like my seawall is broken and water is crashing down around me.

I came upon this Argantian saying when I was trying to write these vows. "Kalon ur wreg zo un delenn; hag a son kaer pa gar un den." A wife's heart is a harp that sounds gently when she loves someone. You are the music that moves my soul. The only absolute truth I've come to believe in is this: I love you.

I'm not a poet, as by now you well know. You once upbraided me for that—for wanting to study stories but never wanting to write any of my own. I couldn't see the point. I thought the only point of scholarship was to uncover the objective meaning, that the best parts of the world were the ones that could be tested and probed, that could be proven true or false. I thought that logic and reason were the only lanterns in the dark.

I remember the moment that I realized it was wrong, all wrong. We were lying side by side in the bed at Penrhos—we'd barely done more than brush hands. I could still hardly admit to myself how badly I wanted to touch you.

You couldn't sleep. You told me how afraid you were, how afraid you'd always been. So we just talked, about some things that didn't matter and some things that did.

I closed my eyes first. I felt you reach over and take my glasses off, setting them down gently on the nightstand. You must have thought I was asleep, but I wasn't. You fell asleep first, and I lay awake there beside you, not thinking, only feeling, and somehow just knowing that this was precisely the right place to be. All the questions, all the frenzied churning of my mind—it all went silent. No contemplating, no theorizing. Just the knowledge that this was right. That I should be with you. It was as unimpeachable as any proven law of nature.

There's not a moment that I've ever doubted it. I loved you then, I loved you now, and I will love you. Always.